A Different Kind Of Cool

By Jeff Conlan

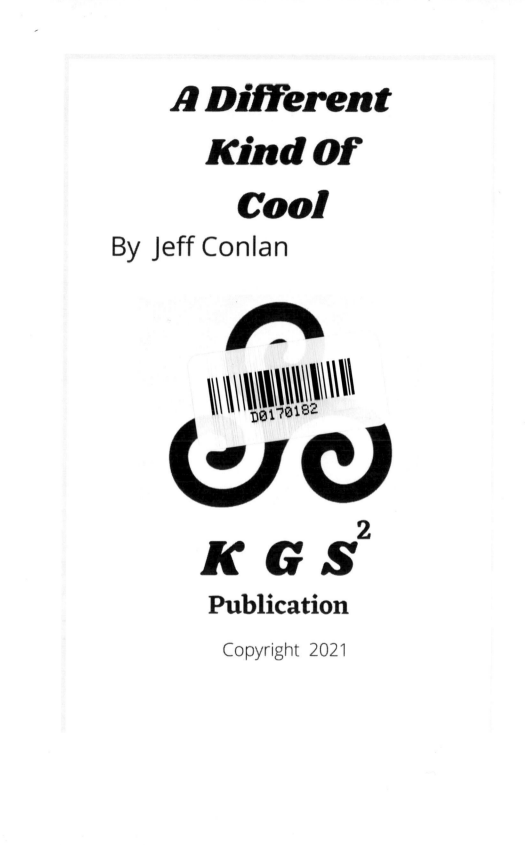

K G S²

Publication

Copyright 2021

Broad-brushes are the tools of fools.

TO WILL,

A beautiful resilient soul. Thank you for giving us a reason to smile and pray every day.

A DIFFERENT KIND OF COOL

Chapters

CHAPTER ONE

Kick-start

Tony Connors grabbed his backpack, threw open the screen door, and jumped down his front steps. He was on his way to see his cousin Wyatt and was running a little late. He never knew how Wyatt was going to be when he got there and running late could definitely get things off on the wrong foot.

Wyatt Rule was not Tony's real cousin, not by blood anyway. Tony and Wyatt's fathers had been best friends growing up. Wyatt was a year older than him. When they were little, Tony remembered trying to do everything just like Wyatt.

One day when they were at the park playing, Tony noticed that some older kids were also doing the same things as Wyatt. They were jumping, flapping their hands, and making noises just like him. Then they started to laugh and point. It did not seem to bother Wyatt in the least. It did however bother Tony. He was only 3 at the time, but he somehow knew it was wrong.

That day changed everything. Tony started noticing differences between him and Wyatt. He asked his mom, "What's wrong with Wyatt?" His mom explained that nothing was wrong with him. Wyatt was autistic and he just saw and experienced things differently than other people. Tony did not fully understand this, but it didn't matter much, he still thought Wyatt was cool.

Tony was older now. He was starting eighth grade in the fall. He understood things much better, including the fact that Wyatt was cool. One thing had changed over the years, Tony had taken on the role of protective brother. Although Wyatt still did not seem to care what other people thought.

When Tony rounded the corner he could see Wyatt on his front porch pacing back and forth, as his service dog, Elvis sat calmly on the top step. He hoped he was not too late. Slight changes in Wyatt's routine without prior notice could throw him off for hours or even days. But when Tony got to the porch Wyatt met him with a big smile.

"Hey, Wyatt." Wyatt did not answer Tony.

He just jumped up and down, made a happy noise, and flipped Tony the football he was holding. Just then Wyatt's mom, June, came out of the house.

"Hello Anthony, you're late," she said.

Tony started to tell her why when she cut him off.

"I'm just kidding, this guy needs to learn to be a little more flexible anyway."

Tony laughed as he started after Wyatt who was already halfway down the block with Elvis by his side, June followed. They were heading three blocks down to the park.

The biggest thing in the small town of Pine Tree was the town park. It was huge and had everything you could imagine a park having. Wyatt loved the park, but sometimes when it was bustling with activity he could become overwhelmed. Tony had seen this happen many times especially when Wyatt was younger. He would seem fine one minute and the next he would be on the ground screaming and crying, sometimes banging his head. It was terrible to watch. People would stare. Even saying ignorant things like, look at that brat. Tony knew better, he knew Wyatt was in some sort of pain. Over the years as Wyatt's parents learned more about autism they were able to notice different warning signs. This allowed them to head off these meltdowns, most of the time.

Tony considered himself an expert at this. He knew when Wyatt was done and needed to leave. It was getting even easier lately. Wyatt, who was very limited verbally, had begun to come up to Tony and say,

" Done, done, done," when he wanted to go.

Tony would smile when Wyatt would do this because he thought it sounded like the dramatic sound effect,

"Dun, dun, duuuun,"

used in old radio shows and comedy sketches.

Tony would say,

"Dun, dun, duuuun," imitating the sound effect.

Sometimes he would get Wyatt to laugh at this. Other times Wyatt would say,

"Done, done, done," again.

To which Tony would reply, "OK, let's go man."

When they arrived at the park, Wyatt would always head straight for the swings. Even now that they were older he still loved to swing. Swinging and swimming always seemed to be his favorite activities. They calmed him in a way nothing else could. Still, Tony was always trying to get Wyatt to try different stuff. He was very into sports and he had seen Wyatt do some amazingly athletic things over the years. This both confused and frustrated him. He knew Wyatt could run faster than any other kid their age, yet he never would if you asked him to. Wyatt was swimming before most kids could walk and was a fish in the water. But most of the time he would just float. One time Tony even saw Wyatt leap like Spider-Man up onto a jungle gym. Run across the entire span and do a backflip off the backend. That was a total one-off and Tony was convinced even his Aunt June, who had her back turned at the time, did not believe him when he told her.

Tony was currently trying to get Wyatt to kick a football. He remembered when they were little Wyatt would sometimes randomly kick his soccer ball with amazing force, especially for a small child. Tony had not had much success as of yet getting Wyatt to kick the ball. So today when they got to the park, Tony laid the football on the ground by Wyatt's feet. He then walked a few feet away and pulled a kicking tee out of his backpack. Tony thought if Wyatt could first watch him kick, it would help. He asked Wyatt to pass him the ball. He was trying to get Wyatt engaged in the activity as fast as possible so he would not lose focus. He had seen his Uncle Billy do this with other tasks and it sometimes worked.

Wyatt passed Tony the ball and said,

"Swing, swing, swing."

"Not yet Wyatt, first, we will kick the ball then swing."

Tony placed the ball on the tee. Elvis looked on with great interest.

"I'll go first, watch Wyatt."

When he saw he had Wyatt's attention, he took two steps back from the ball and two steps to the side. Tony announced this aloud as he did it.

"Two steps back Wyatt, two steps to the side. Then just step and kick".

Tony took three strides towards the ball and kicked. The ball flew in the air and Elvis immediately began to track it.

June saw this and yelled to him,

"Elvis gentle, gentle Elvis."

This was actually one of Elvis's command words. Hearing this Elvis picked the ball up with great care and proudly trotted back toward Tony and Wyatt.

When he reached them Tony said,

"Elvis, drop it",

Elvis dropped the ball at Tony's feet. Tony gave Elvis great praise, "Great job boy".

He picked the ball back up, which aside from a few more teeth marks, was no worse for wear. He turned to Wyatt, who was getting a little more anxious now.

"Your turn, Wyatt."

Tony placed the ball back on the tee.

"Come on Wyatt you can do it, just give it a kick it's fun."

Wyatt approached the ball and barely gave it a nudge off the tee.

"Come on man, I know you can do better than that."

He placed the ball on the tee again. This time Wyatt ran up, picked the ball off the tee, and punched it like a volleyball.

Then jumped up in the air yelling, "AHHHH," and started laughing.

Tony looked at Wyatt and said, "Come on Wyatt, give me one kick today."

Tony turned and picked the ball up off the ground, which Elvis had already dropped at his feet without any commands. Tony placed the ball back on the tee and said,

"Come on Wyatt, one good kick and then the swings".

Wyatt approached the ball and then backed up 3 steps. Tony looked on with excitement. Wyatt took 3 strides towards the ball, cocked his leg back, but pulled up just short of kicking it.

Tony looked at him and Wyatt was giving him this little side smile. Tony started to laugh and said,

"Oh, a wise guy hey."

Wyatt laughed hard as he flayed his body around. Tony loved these interactions with Wyatt, not many people knew it, but the kid had a very good sense of humor.

"Okay, I can see this is going nowhere, let's go to the swings."

Tony bent down to pick up the ball and tee. Wyatt grabbed his arm and in a more serious tone said,

"OK, OK, OK".

Tony said, "Really? Go ahead then."

This time Wyatt took one step back off the ball. Then with one stride back towards the ball, he gave it a half-hearted kick. The ball flew in the air end over end landing about 60 feet away. Elvis almost beat it to the spot.

Tony yelled with excitement,

"That was great, Wyatt, would have been a good extra point in the old NFL. Now imagine if you used all your strength."

Tony snatched up the tee. Elvis stood there with the ball in his mouth as if he knew they were done here. Wyatt took off towards the swings and Elvis took off after him.

Tony said, "Wait up."

He saw his Aunt June up ahead texting on her phone. She seemed to have a knack for anticipating Wyatt's next move.

When he caught up to them Tony asked his Aunt,

"Did you see Wyatt kick the ball?"

June said, "Yes Anthony, that was great! I could never get him to do that."

Tony said, "Yeah it was a pretty good kick. I'm starting football in the Fall, maybe if we keep working at it, Wyatt could be the kicker."

June smiled, "We'll see Anthony, but don't get your hopes up."

Tony laughed, "I know."

After playing in the park they headed back toward the house. When they got to the last stretch of sidewalk, Wyatt took off in a sprint like he always did yelling happily with Elvis by his side.

Tony could see his Uncle Billy in front of the house working on something. Uncle Billy gave Wyatt a high five as Wyatt and Elvis quickly ran past him on their way into the house. Tony and June arrived a few seconds later.

"Hey Uncle Billy," said Tony.

"What's up Anthony?" he replied.

"Not much, I got Wyatt to kick the ball today."

"That's great, good job, how far did he kick it?"

"He kicked it about sixty feet without even trying."

"Yeah, that doesn't surprise me."

June interrupted, "Speaking of surprises, I can't believe what I'm seeing. You're finally fixing this old lamp post?"

"Well I do everything else, so I figured I'd knock this out too," said Billy with a sarcastic face.

"Yeah right, I'd better get inside before Wyatt feeds everything in the fridge to Elvis. I'll see you later Anthony, great job with Wyatt today." June headed into the house.

"So your dad said you're starting football this year? No more soccer?" asked Billy.

"Yeah, I've been thinking about playing for a while. But there's a lot of pressure, everybody expects me to be awesome. In case you don't remember, you guys are legends around here."

"Oh please, that's nonsense. Just practice hard and play hard. You'll do just fine. Don't worry about what anyone else says. Besides, I've seen the way you move especially for a big kid. You don't have anything to worry about. I am surprised your dad hasn't tried to get you into wrestling though."

Tony laughed, "He tries all the time, but I like basketball too much."

Uncle Billy smiled, "I was the same way, I might have given wrestling a shot growing up if it wasn't the same season as basketball."

"Hey Uncle Billy, do you think Wyatt could maybe be part of the team? I know that he probably wouldn't be able to play in games or anything, but I thought maybe he would like to go to practices and stuff. He knows a lot of the guys. Everybody likes Wyatt, he's a different kind of cool. Who knows, maybe he could even kick?"

"A different kind of cool," Billy repeated with a smile. "I don't know Anthony, let me talk to your Aunt June first. We'd have to talk to the coach. Then see if Wyatt even has any interest. If he did, we'd have to get an aide to go with him, we'll see."

"Okay, it's just an idea," said Tony.

"It's a good idea, we'll see if we can work it out."

Tony smiled, "Oh, I almost forgot. My dad told me to tell you that Glenn called him last night. He said he's coming in next Saturday and he has big news. Dad said if you want, text him later because he's working at the bar and he won't be able to hear you on the phone. But he knows you hate to text."

Billy laughed, "He's right I'll call him tomorrow. And Anthony, remember what I told you. Forget all those ancient stories about your dad, Glenn, and me. Most of them are exaggerated anyway. You're gonna do just fine."

"Thanks, Uncle Billy, maybe I'll see you tomorrow."

"Alright Anthony, see you later buddy."

The next day Billy Rule called Jack Connors to see what was going on with Glenn. Glenn Gilmore had completed their trio growing up, they were inseparable. Glenn had gone on to play professional football. He often came back to Pine Tree to visit his parents and the guys. Much of the town park amenities were paid for by Glenn, but he always insisted on remaining anonymous. Glenn still lived in California where he had played most of his career.

Jack answered on the third ring. "Hey, Billy what's up man?"

"I don't know, you tell me, Anthony said Glenn was coming in and had some big news?" answered Billy.

"Yeah, he says he's done with the sun and he's moving back to Pine Tree. Off the record, he's buying the High school a brand new field, with new lights, new everything. Here's the best part the current varsity coach is leaving after this year and guess who's taking his place?"

"John Candy?" said Billy with a smile in his voice.

"Very funny, no, Glenn."

"Wow, Nancy and the kids are good with that?"

"He said Nancy has always loved it here and the twins are starting college next year. Besides, he's keeping his other houses."

"Right, the other houses," Billy said and they both laughed.

"Hey what's this Anthony tells me, Wyatts going to practice with the team?"

"Oh I don't know, I'll have to talk to the coach. We like getting Wyatt around the other kids as much as possible. So if Wyatt wants to and the coach will do it, maybe they can find a spot for him. This is all Anthony's idea, you know? He's always been great with Wyatt so I'm willing to run with it."

"Well I don't think the coach is going to be an issue, it's Tim Houzer," said Jack.

"You're kidding me, that's great. I haven't seen Tim a lot since we graduated. He's always been a good dude. June will be glad to hear it's someone we know."

"Well I hope it works out, I gotta run. I'll talk to you later," said Jack.

"Yeah Jack, sounds good, later man." Billy hung up the phone.

He sat back in his chair. June had taken Wyatt to OT, the house was quiet. His eyes drifted up and fixed upon the team photo he had on the wall of the 1990 Pine Tree Eagles football team. Billy had not thought about his so-called glory days in a long time. Sure other people would bring them up, but it always seemed like they were talking about someone else as if it never really happened. Sitting there in his den it all came flooding back.

CHAPTER TWO

Glory Days

Billy Rule, Jack Connors, and Glenn Gilmore were the three best athletes that the town of Pine Tree ever had. You would be lucky to see one athlete as gifted come through a small town, to have three the same age was nothing short of a miracle. At least that's the way the townspeople saw it.

From the time they met in kindergarten, they were inseparable. Playing for hours in the old town park. Back then, it was mostly woods and a few fields carved out of an old dirt race track that closed in the early 1960s.

When the boys were twelve. Mr. Gilmore, who was a very successful construction contractor, approached the town about improving the park. He offered to cover the labor costs if the town would pay for the materials. The town agreed. Mr. Gilmore built new fields, courts, and playgrounds. Before long all the kids in the town were playing and practicing there.

That was the same year he finagled stadium lighting from a job he was doing at the state prison. He recruited Billy's dad, who was an electrician, and a few other friends from the town who were linemen to rig up the lights for the High School football field. Pine Tree was the first school in the region to have lights. Even the well-to-do neighboring town, the dreaded Walnut Heights, did not have lights.

Walnut Heights had long been a football factory. Crushing Pine Tree and winning the Regional Bowl game was an annual event. Mr. Gilmore was a shrewd businessman who hated losing. Along with the Pine Tree school district, he negotiated a deal with Walnut Heights and every other school in the area. They would be able to use the newly lighted field for their championship games and any other special events, for a fee of course.

He also had an eye for real talent. His son and his two friends were the real deal. Walnut Heights didn't know it yet, but they had a challenge coming, and that eye-opening game would be played under the lights on Pine Tree's home field.

Mr. Gilmore had not been sitting home at night twisting his mustache, thinking about eventually beating Walnut Heights. He just wanted to make sure it was an equal playing field. As the boys grew older, his plan seemed to be falling into place. They were all excelling both in school and on the field.

Billy Rule was tall, lean, and fast as lightning. He played outside linebacker and wide receiver on the football team. He was an All-State sprinter and an All-County linebacker by his Junior year. Jack Connors was not quite as tall as Billy but he was extremely strong. He had long arms and a torso with short powerful legs. Jack was an All-State defensive end, receiving the same honors in both the shot put and discus. However, his main sport was wrestling. Jack would go on to win the state championship at 215 lbs his junior year and the 250 lb title his senior year.

As amazing as both Billy and Jack's resumes were, there was just something different about Glenn Gilmore. Glenn worked just as hard as his friends or at least he pretended to.

Billy once asked Jack when Glenn wasn't around.

"Do you ever get the feeling that Glenn is holding back in order to fit in? It's as if he doesn't want us to find out that he's Superman."

"I think Superman knows and he's worried Glenn is gonna take his job," answered Jack.

It was true, everything seemed to come easy to him. Even in school, he was top of his class. Glenn looked like a quarterback from central casting and lived up to all the hype. He could have been anything. He settled for being the best quarterback and pitcher in the state if not the country by his senior year.

In their sophomore year, the boys and the rest of the Pine Tree Eagles were not quite on par with Walnut Heights. They lost to them in the regular season at home under the lights. It was a close game. Glenn threw for over 300 yards and 3 touchdowns, which would have been great in any High school game, but was unheard of against Walnut Heights. Billy caught two of those TDs and Jack had 4 sacks. The final score was 28-24, and Walnut Heights definitely took notice.

Two games later in the snow, Pine Tree would admittingly take a solid Hudson Ridge team lightly and lose 12-6. Some thought that game should not have been played in those conditions, especially Mr. Gilmore who was furious about it.

That loss knocked them out of bowl contention. The boys sat in the stands and watched Walnut Heights destroy Hudson Ridge in the Regional Bowl game on Pine Trees' home field 42-10. Walnut Heights won another State Championship that year.

In their junior year, they played Walnut Heights to a 28-28 tie during the regular season. The game was played in Walnut Heights and to say that there was some home cooking going on with the refs would be an understatement.

Despite the tie, Pine Tree made it to their first bowl game appearance in 25 years. It appeared to many people that this could be Pine Tree's year. What they did not know was that the summer before, Walnut Heights had deployed a secret weapon. And it came in the shape of the Spencer twins.

Heidi and Holly Spencer were going into their senior year at Walnut Heights. When they met Jack Connors and Glenn Gilmore on the Million dollar beach in Lake George. It's long since been an urban legend. That was no chance meeting, but the fact is nobody could have predicted what would happen next.

Jack and Glenn started dating the Spencer twins which was all anyone under the age of 18 talked about aside from football. Billy had not been hanging out as much that summer. He spent most of his spare time helping his dad with his electrical business. That probably spared him from what happened next.

Two weeks before the bowl game the Spencer twins came down with Mono. One week later, so did Jack Connors and Glenn Gilmore. Neither could play in the game. It was later dubbed the " Spencer Bowl."

Billy Rule put on a hell of a show in that game. The Pine Tree Coach, Gus Parker, had Billy practice at running back for the week leading up to it. He would rush for over 200 yards and score 4 TDs. All in a losing effort. Pine Tree fell again to Walnut Heights 35-28.

Billy would never let the guys forget that loss. But he knew he really could not blame them. He had seen the Spencer twins. It also more than likely helped him get a full ride to the University of Michigan. There had been scouts at the game to watch Glenn. It seemed to slip old Coach Parker's mind to inform all of them that Glenn would not be playing.

The mission of defeating Walnut Heights would come down to their senior year. In Mr. Gilmore's mind, nothing was going to stop them that year.

The boys knew it was not going to be easy. Outside of the three of them, their team was a lot weaker than in previous years. They had graduated a lot of good players, but because they were so good people seemed to overlook that fact. The boys never did, they always let their teammates know how important they were.

That year the only other senior was Tim Houzer, a nice guy who played hard but was not a gifted athlete. Walnut Heights on the other hand was loaded, even for them.

They had an all-state Quarterback in Brice Cooper and an All-American running back, Terry Brooks, who was on his way to Florida State. The rest of their starting lineup consisted mostly of seniors. Still, the boys were confident they could beat them.

Pine Tree was not scheduled to play Walnut Heights until the third to last game of the season. It turned out there was a snowstorm that week and the game was canceled. It was never made up. Since both teams were undefeated at the end of the season, they simply moved on to the Regional Bowl game.

The day of the game was insane. People from all over packed

into Pine Tree, including national news outlets. Some of Glenn's highlights had been on, " The George Michael Sports Machine" show, which back in the day before the internet was a big deal. This drew even more attention to a game that was already highly touted.

Traffic was getting bad in town. It was decided to get both teams to the school by 2 pm for an 8 o'clock start. To kill time, some of the assistant coaches took a pitching wedge out to the field and worked on their golf game. That was until Coach Parker saw them and lost his mind. He berated them for messing up the field. Coach Parker was usually a mild-mannered man, but tensions were running high. When the teams finally took the field even the players from Walnut Heights could not believe their eyes, it was beyond packed, you would have thought it was the Orange Bowl.

Walnut Heights won the toss and chose to receive the ball. Billy Rule flew down the field on the opening kickoff and buried the return man at the 15. The crowd erupted.

Before Billy and Jack went back on defense Glenn quickly ran up and said to them,

"Hey, you guys see who's in the stands?"

Jack replied, "Who, John Candy?" They all laughed.

"No," Glenn said, "Heidi and Holly, and it looks like they brought some friends back from Ohio state. Maybe we can celebrate with them after we win."

Billy said, "Great, bad enough they're from Walnut Heights, now they go to Ohio State. I'm going to Michigan next year, remember?"

"What better story for the guys at Michigan, hell their boy-friends probably play for Ohio State," said Jack. They all laughed again.

"Fast and loose guys, let's go, we got this," Glenn yelled as Billy and Jack returned to the field.

Walnut Heights was not buying the hype. They started a methodical march down the field. It was second and 8 on Pine Tree's 45 when Walnut Heights', Terry Brooks broke a 30 yard run down to the 15.

Jack went over to Billy,

"I got a real good read on the snap count. I'm going to jump it this time, be ready."

Billy said, "I got it, brother."

Well, Jack was not kidding, he timed it perfectly hitting the QB, so hard and fast he had no time to protect the ball. Unfortunately, Billy did not come up with it. Instead, it went right into the arms of Tim Houzer. Tim seemed to freeze for a second until he must have heard Billy and Jack yelling at him RUUUN!! Tim took off down the field with Billy just off his wing blocking.

Tim kept yelling to Billy, "DO YOU WANT THE BALL? DO YOU WANT THE BALL!!" for the entire 80 yards.

Billy just kept yelling back, " JUST RUN TIM, RUN!".

Tim Houzer had never scored a touchdown in his life. Now he

had just run a ball back 80 yards for the first score in the biggest game in town history. The crowd was going crazy.

Tim said to Billy on the sideline,

"Why didn't you take the ball?"

Billy replied, "Are you kidding, you were running so fast I could barely keep up."

Tim laughed, "Yeah Right."

The rest of the game went back and forth. Walnut Heights knew that aside from Jack and Billy the Pine Tree defense was not much of a threat. Walnut Heights was having an equally tough time stopping Glenn and the Pine Tree offense. At halftime, the score was tied at 21.

Pine Tree had a few nice drives in the third quarter, but they were stopped short of getting in the endzone and missed two field goals. Brooks broke another long run for a TD right at the end of the third. Walnut Heights's wideout who was also their kicker was roughed up on the play. They had no one else to kick the extra point. So they went for a 2 point conversion and got it, putting Walnut Heights up 29-21 going into the fourth.

Then Coach Parker tried something they had not done in a game all year. He put Jack in at fullback to open up a hole for Billy. The idea worked, Jack blew open a huge hole and Billy flew right through it for a 53 yard TD run. They went for 2 in order to tie it up. Glenn took the snap and rolled out to his right as if he was going to try and loft one to Billy in the corner of the endzone. Instead, he threw back across his body and hit sophomore receiver Bobby Niles with a perfect pass which went right through his hands. The score was now Walnut Heights 29 Pine Tree 27.

The next few drives for both teams stalled. Walnut Heights got the ball back with 3:33 left in the game. They started to whittle down the clock by handing the ball off to Brooks. He was able to get a first down with 2:29 left with the ball on Pine Trees 43 yard line. Then on the next play, Cooper took everyone by surprise when he dropped back and hit the tight end down the middle of the field for a 35 yard gain. Billy delivered a punishing hit, but the damage was done. Pine Tree called an immediate time-out. It was first and goal with 2:24 left to go.

Jack went over to Billy, "Damn, I didn't expect that."

Billy replied, "Me neither".

Jack said, "Listen we obviously need to do something right now. They've been mixing up the count pretty well but I'm going to jump it anyway. And Billy, this time, try to come up with the ball if I knock it loose. I love Tim, but I think he'll have a heart attack if he gets the ball again."

Billy laughed and said, "I'll do my best brother."

The next play seemed to happen in slow motion. Jack's timing was perfect. He hit Cooper before he could hand the ball off to Brooks. It miraculously bounced off the turf directly to Billy. At that moment, everyone there knew the game was over. There was no one in the state who could catch Billy Rule with an open field in front of him. He took off like a rocket. The sound of the crowd was just one big roar. When he got near the Walnut Heights 20 yard line he started to smile. It was pure joy, and that's when at full stride he stepped into a divot made by a pitching wedge before the game. His knee exploded. Billy went down as if he had been shot.

He held onto the ball and Terry Brooks who was 10 yards behind him started waving for help.

Billy could not believe what was happening, he knew his knee was destroyed. The coaches and trainers wanted to have the paramedics take Billy off the field on a stretcher. Billy refused and said he could walk off. The pain had subsided but his knee was already starting to swell. Mr. Rule had made his way onto the field and gave his permission to let Billy walk-off if he could.

Mr. Rule said to Billy, "Listen, if you want to walk off that's fine. But then you're going straight to my car and to the hospital to get that looked at, and I don't want to hear anything else about it."

Billy agreed and Jack and Glenn helped him to his feet. The crowd cheered, including Walnut Heights fans.

Billy said to the guys, "I can't believe this, it feels like some horrible dream."

Glenn replied, "Maybe it's not that bad."

Billy said, "It's bad, It's really bad. I've never felt anything close to that."

Jack chimed in, "Well you won't know until the doctors look at it. Cheer up man you just won this game for us. We're in scoring position."

Jack and Glenn helped Billy onto the bench. Jack sat next to him and Glenn ran back onto the field. Glenn was not gone long as Pine Tree failed to get a first down. Without Walnut Heights worrying about Billy they tightened down their defense. Pine Tree would have to try for a field goal. They called timeout and Glenn sat down next to Jack and Billy.

"Well, I guess you guys can put your Superman theory to rest," said Glenn.

They both looked at him, Billy said, "How'd you know about that?"

Glenn said, "I just meant that everybody acts like I'm Superman, why, you have a theory?"

They both said, "NO", at the same time.

Glenn looked at them,

"You guys are idiots."

Jack changed the subject,

"We still got this, all Frank has to do is hit, what, a 30 yarder? He can kick that in his sleep."

Nobody replied, their collective silence was due to the fact that they did not have great confidence in Frank Reilly at the time. Frank was a junior and had a good leg, but lately, he was in a slump. He already missed two FGs in the game. One from 45 the other from 33. The ball was on the 24-yard line, which would make it a 41 yard FG on what was becoming a pretty chilly night. It definitely was not a chip shot, especially for a High School kicker under a lot of pressure.

Glenn got up, "Well I better get back out there." He ran back out onto the field.

Mr. Rule was on Billy's case by now to go to his car so they wouldn't get stuck in traffic. Billy knew one of the paramedics who had been a couple of years ahead of him in school. Billy had him assure Mr. Rule that they would take both of them directly to the hospital right after the kick, lights, and siren. Mr. Rule agreed as the players lined up for the FG attempt.

Glenn was the holder for Frank, the crowd was so loud he had to yell to him before they lined up.

He said with a big smile,

"Frank, no pressure, it's just like practice."

Frank started laughing and said,

"Oh yeah, no worries."

The snap was a little high, but Glenn quickly corrected it for a good hold. Frank hit the ball solid with plenty of leg. The ball hooked left and slammed off the upright with a loud gong sound and careened out of bounds, no good.

Walnut Heights got the ball back and uneventfully ran out the clock. The town of Pine Tree was in shock. The boys would move on from the loss but they would never forget how close they came.

Jack Connors would go on to have a great collegiate wrestling career at Oklahoma State. Glenn Gilmore went on to Notre Dame and won a National Championship in his Junior year and the Heisman Trophy in his senior year. He would later get drafted number one overall. Michigan honored Billy's scholarship. But at the time knee surgeries were not what they are today. He never regained his speed and before his sophomore year, they pulled his scholarship. He returned to Pine Tree and went to work for his father as an electrician.

The year after the Bowl game Walnut Heights installed a new turf field and modern stadium lighting. All the Regional Bowl games would move to the new venue, and with the boys graduating, Pine Tree moved back into obscurity.

CHAPTER THREE

Billy and June

June Slevin grew up in the town of Hudson Ridge. A small town along a very narrow section of the Hudson River some 200 hundred miles north of NYC. It bordered Pine Tree to the east and Walnut Heights to the south. June's father owned the biggest electrical supply house in the county. She had worked in the store off and on over the years. After college, she put her business degree to work and took on a more active role. Her older brother Tommy ran the warehouse well, but balancing the books was not his strong point. Mr. Slevin was still running the store, although by the spring of 1997 he had begun talking about retirement. June had big plans, she saw a great opportunity to expand the operation. She wanted to open another store or two.

Billy was five years removed from cutting ties with Michigan. He had been working full-time alongside his father. Mr. Rule had been battling cancer for years and recently he had taken a turn for the worse. Billy was a very capable electrician and his father had assembled a good crew over the years. Nobody seemed to have a problem with Billy running the day-to-day. Besides, the business had actually picked up since he had. He was a legend in these parts.

Billy would always smile and nod his head when people would tell their stories about this game or that game, but it made him feel like he was a hundred years old. Pat Connors, Jack's older brother, was part of the work crew. He knew Billy wasn't a big fan of the constant glory days conversations. So he would tease him about it.

He would say, "BILLY, Billy Rule, wow that is you? I saw you run for 500 yards and 10 TDs against the Heights. Shame what happened to you. How is the knee?"

To which Billy would smile and say,

"Screw you, Pat."

Billy and Pat were taking a ride into Hudson Ridge on a Saturday morning. They were on their way to Slevin's to order supplies for a big job they had. Billy always loved going to Slevin's growing up. It was a cool old building that had been a mill for years before the Slevin family bought it in the 1930s. Originally it was Slevin's Hardware, before the current owner John Slevin had turned it into an electrical supply warehouse. They still sold some hardware and other general store items.

Mr. Rule would take Billy with him sometimes on his trips to Slevins. The store always smelled so good. In the winter the wood stove would be burning and for whatever reason, it smelled better than anywhere else. Billy's dad told him that was because the Slevins burned Cherry wood. In the summer and fall, Mrs. Slevin would bake pies and cookies that they sold at the store. Whenever Billy would see Norman Rockwell paintings he thought of Slevins. One day when Billy was about six he was running around in the aisles. He came around a corner and was suddenly face to face with a little girl who was about his age, maybe a little younger. Neither of them said anything. They just stared at each other for a short time. Billy remembered that he got a warm tingling feeling that ran up his back and the hair stood up on his arms. Then as quickly as she was there she was gone. She turned and ran through the swinging doors to the back of the store. Billy never forgot that little girl. And from time to time he would see her on his trips to Slevins. She was John Slevin's youngest daughter, June.

Billy was not shy around girls but for some reason over the years the best he could ever muster when he saw June was "Hello". Jack and Glenn knew about June when they were growing up. Billy must have let it slip one time. They would occasionally poke fun at his fascination with her. Pat also knew about her, he made it his business to know stuff like that. He was a good guy, but he loved to bust chops.

When Billy and Pat pulled up to Slevin's, Mr. Slevin was standing out front. Pat got out of the van first and said,

"Hi, John" to Mr. Slevin, as he walked up the front porch steps past him.

Mr. Slevin said, "Good morning Pat".

Billy got out and closed the door to the van.

"Good Morning, Mr. Slevin."

"Good Morning Billy, how's your Pop doing?"

Billy bit down on his lip for a second and made a face as if to say not good, then replied,

"He's hanging in there, still fighting."

"So sorry Billy, I know I don't have to tell you this, but your dad is a great man."

"Thanks, Mr. Slevin, I'll let him know you were asking about him."

Billy walked up the steps next to Pat. Mr. Slevin looked up at them and said,

"Whatever you guys need, June is inside she can help you."

Billy and Pat said," Thank you," at the same time as they walked into the store.

 Pat was now behind Billy and he whispered in his ear,

"Now's your big chance. He just offered up June."

Billy shook his head, "Shut up man, you're such an ass."

Pat was laughing.

Billy said, "I'm glad you're enjoying yourself, you can put the order in."

 Pat shook his head,

"Oh no, you're not weaseling out of this one."

Pat cleared his throat extra loud, June looked up from the parts computer on the counter.

"Hey, guys.' Sorry, I didn't hear you come in".

"That's okay June, Billy here has a big order to place. He'll fill you in on all the details. Can I use your bathroom?"

Pat started to head for the bathroom before June could even answer. He gave a quick look back at Billy with a big grin on his face. Billy wanted to kill him.

"Hi Billy, so sorry to hear about your Dad. He's such a nice man," said June.

"Thank you," Billy replied awkwardly.

He knew in his head that he was acting odd but he couldn't help it. He was staring at June now without saying anything.

"Do you have a list of supplies or do you want to just tell me what you need?" said June, breaking the silence.

Billy snapped out of it.

"Of course, sorry, I have a list here. I don't need it until the end of next week but I just wanted to give you guys time. It's a lot of material."

"Sure, just give me the list. I can run it right now, see what we have."

Billy stepped closer and handed her the list. Damn, she smelled good, Billy thought. He laughed in his head, everything smells good at Slevins.

June was typing very fast on the parts computer. She looked up at Billy,

"It looks like we have everything in stock. But I'm glad you came early so I can reorder. Let me just check and see if we have all this 12/3 Romex."

June came from behind the counter and walked past Billy down one of the long isles. She had on an old 3/4 sleeve t-shirt, blue jeans, and work boots. Billy thought she was so hot, he wondered if she knew that she was driving him crazy.

"Yeah, so we have some here, and I show that we have more in the back. I can have this whole order ready for delivery or pick up first thing Monday morning," said June as she walked back past Billy.

"That's great, I'll send some of the guy's to pick it up on Monday then, thanks June."

"No problem, thank you. Tell your dad I said hello, I pray he gets better."

"I will, thanks again."

Billy turned and walked out the door. He could see Pat was sitting in the driver's seat of the van. Billy opened the passenger's door and jumped in.

"What's up Pat I thought you said I was a terrible passenger? Now all of a sudden you want to drive?"

"I don't want to drive, but we're not leaving until you ask June out," said Pat.

"What, are you crazy? Get the hell out of here Pat, start the freakin' van."

"I can't believe you're such a chicken shit. One of these days you're gonna walk in there and she's going to have a ring on her finger. And sure, you'll act all cool like you don't care. But you will be full of crap, just like you are now."

Billy stared at Pat for a few seconds, he had to handle this situation correctly. Most people would think Pat was just joking around at this point, but Billy knew Pat was only half kidding. Pat was a strange bird and this could easily turn into the two of them rolling around fighting in the parking lot if he didn't say the right thing.

"Listen, first off, it's none of your business, sure I think she's cute. But if I ask her out and it doesn't go well in the short term, or long term it could have an effect on our business relationship. And in case you forgot, Slevin's is the only electrical supply in a hundred miles. So start the van, Cupid, and let's get out of here. Besides, she has a boyfriend."

Pat cracked up laughing.

"You are so full of crap, and I just talked to her brother Tommy in the back. She doesn't have a boyfriend. And he would love it if she did because she's driving him nuts. So get your sorry ass back in there and ask her out. Ask her to Jack's grand opening next weekend, it would be perfect."

They sat in silence for a minute. Then Pat said,

"I don't know what you're waiting for."

Billy did not say anything, he got back out of the van and

slammed the door. For some reason he knew Pat was right, maybe it was just the push he needed. He was going to finally ask June Slevin out. He marched back up the stairs and through the door. June was behind the counter and looked up when he came back in.

"Oh hey Billy, did you forget something?"

Billy hesitated for a second and then said,

"June, do you want to go out with me next Saturday? My friend Jack is opening a new bar and I figured you might want to go and Pat's busting my stones about asking you out. He said Tommy said that you didn't have a boyfriend. Not that I'm asking you out just because of Pat. The truth is I've been wanting to ask you out forever and I don't know why I haven't. So do you want to go out next Saturday, if not no worries, that's cool? And I'll just send some of the guys over Monday to pick up the order."

June had a surprised look on her face. Billy closed his eyes for half a second and thought to himself, I am such a loser. Pat is dead.

Then June smiled and said,

"Wow, that's a lot. I would love to go with you, Billy." She was laughing a little.

Billy started to laugh now too, he said,

"That was the most awkward thing ever, I'm sorry. Really if you don't want to go, don't worry about it."

June was still smiling.

"No, I want to go, Billy, it would be great. I have not done anything fun in a long time. Here, take my home number and let me know when and where."

Billy walked up to the counter and took the number from June.

"Great, I'm gonna go now for real before I start yammering on again. I'll call you during the week, June, it was nice to see you."

Billy turned and walked out of the store. He felt light-headed, he had a huge smile on his face. Pat was sitting back on the passenger's side. Billy got back into the driver's seat and closed the door. He looked over at Pat. Pat continued looking straight ahead and said,

"I don't know what you're smiling about, you're gonna screw it up. And Slevin's is the only Electrical supply, in a hundred miles."

Billy started laughing,

"You are such an asshole."

Pat smiled and replied,

"Thanks, and you're welcome."

June went with Billy to the grand opening of "Connors Welcome Inn". Jack with some help from Mr. Gilmore had renovated an old Inn that was across from the Pine Tree train station. They could see a line of people out front, Billy parked around back.

"Well this is it, Jack told me that we should come in through the back."

"The place looks great, I can't wait to see the inside," June replied.

They got out of the car and started to walk towards the back of the Inn when they heard a voice.

"Hey, Billy." Billy knew right away that it was Glenn.

They turned and saw Glenn getting out of a beautiful classic 1969 Chevy Blazer. He was wearing a Notre Dame baseball cap tilted up on his head, a flannel shirt open with a white t-shirt underneath, blue jeans, and brown Doc Martens. Doing his best to blend in and failing miserably, he still looked better than any movie star even in real life.

"Hey Glenn, what's up man? Jack said he didn't think you were going to make it," Billy said with a smile.

"You know me, brother, I just wanted to surprise him. I wouldn't miss this. Besides, it will be nice to skip out on a big tab later," Glenn said as he shook Billy's hand.

Billy laughed, "Who are you kidding? I heard you floated him the money for this place."

Glenn was not looking at Billy anymore; his eyes were fixed on June.

"Rumors Billy, just rumors, Hi I'm Glenn Gilmore," he said to June.

June smiled and said, "I know, I'm June Slevin, nice to meet you, Glenn."

Glenn's face became animated, he smiled big and shook June's hand while covering it with the other.

"Holy Shit, you're June Slevin? This is awesome."

Billy was smiling and shaking his head. Glenn continued.

"Forgive me but we weren't sure you existed. Billy's been talking about you since I can't remember. Wow, this is great, how long have you two been dating?"

Billy cleared his throat and said,

"This is our first date Glenn, and now that you've exposed me as a giant stalker, probably our last. Thanks, buddy."

June laughed, "Don't worry Glenn, Billy already exposed himself as a giant stalker when he asked me out."

"Come on stalker is a little harsh. I admired you from afar, besides I caught you checking me out over the years."

The stalker jokes continued as the three of them made their way up the iron stairs that led to the rear of the second floor. They went inside and walked down a long hallway that ended at a wraparound balcony overlooking the main bar room.

Billy saw Jack standing at the end of the bar talking to someone. He waved his arm to catch Jack's attention. Jack saw him and waved for him to come down. Billy pointed to Glenn. Jack smiled and put his finger up as if to say one minute. Billy and Jack knew that Glenn would be swarmed if he walked down through the crowd. After all, he was only 3 months removed from winning his first Super Bowl.

Glenn caught on and said,

"Oh screw this, I'm not going VIP in my hometown."

He walked past Billy and June down the stairs into the bar. Billy looked at June, shrugged, took her hand, and followed Glenn down. Jack met them at the bottom of the stairs.

"I knew you'd make it", Jack said to Glenn. "I have a table set up in the back corner for everyone. If we can get Glenn through the crowd."

Glenn rolled his eyes," Guys relax, this is still Pine Tree. Not L.A. or Manhattan, I think I can handle it."

Then he drifted right through the crowd with a few smiles and handshakes and found his way to the table.

Jack had a long table set up that ended with a big horseshoe booth. Billy was surprised to see his Mom and Dad sitting in the middle of the booth. Billy, June, and Glenn slid in next to them. Mr. Rule was talking to someone on the other side.

Billy said to his Mom, "I'm surprised he made it, is he okay?"

His Mom said, "He was feeling good and he wanted to go, so I wasn't going to argue with him."

Billy nodded, "Well I guess there's a first time for everything," he gave his mom a little nudge to show he was kidding.

His mom gave him a dismissive look and said,

"June it's so nice to see you. When Billy said he was bringing you I couldn't believe it. I thought he'd never get off his butt and ask you out."

Billy put his head in his hand and leaned over and whispered to June.

"This was probably a bad idea for a first date. If you can find it in your heart to give me a second chance, I'll do better."

"Are you kidding, this is great, to find out that Billy Rule, one of the Pine Tree Three, has been pining over me all these years, I think I'll survive."

Billy smirked,

"Well, don't get too big of a head, I'm pretty sure I am the low man on that Totem pole."

June leaned in, looked Billy in the eye, and said,

"I don't think so."

Billy felt that warm tingling feeling run up his back and the hair stood up on his arms. Just then Glenn tapped him on the shoulder and asked him,

"What do you guys want to drink?"

The rest of the night went great, they hardly got up from the table. Billy even joked to Glenn that it was like being the host on a talk show. Different people just kept getting in and out of the booth and talking to them all night. Billy knew June had to open the store in the morning. So before it got too late he told Glenn that they were going to do an Irish goodbye and sneak out through the kitchen. Glenn said he would run interference. He got up and walked towards the bar. Billy and June beat it through the kitchen and out the side of the Inn. They were talking about the night as Billy drove June home. It got quiet for a minute so Billy pushed a tape into the car stereo. The song "Red Cortina" by The Saw Doctors, started to play. They listened for a while and June said,

"This is good, who is it?"

"The Saw Doctors," Billy replied.

"Really? It doesn't sound like them at all."

Billy chuckled and said," The Saw Doctors, not the Spin Doctors. They're an Irish rock band, Jack's sister brought a tape home from Ireland one summer and we've all been listening to them ever since."

June was swaying to the music,

"I like them, I don't think I've ever really listened to Irish rock before except for U2."

Billy laughed again,

"Yeah I like U2 also, but this is totally different. You should go with us this year to the Irish festival in the Catskills. They play there some years, it's a lot of fun."

June put her hand on top of Billy's which was resting on the middle console.

"Sounds cool, maybe I will, I think my brother Tommy has gone a few times."

They drove in silence again as the song "N17" played. June broke the silence,

"Your Mom is a riot, she was cracking me up. She told me that you could remember the first time you saw me."

Billy exhaled and said,

"Boy, I'm never gonna live this stuff down, what a bunch of rats, payback is definitely coming."

"I thought it was cute," June said as they pulled into her driveway.

Billy put the car in park.

"Well, I don't know if cute is really what I'm going for."

"Oh yeah, what exactly are you going for?" said June.

Billy smiled and said,

"Can I kiss you?"

June smiled back,

"You'd better."

They kissed for a short time and then June said,

"I'd better go in, it's getting late."

June got out of the car and then leaned back in,

"Billy I remember the first time I saw you too. It was in the store, I was about 5 and we almost ran into each other. You were wearing a yellow shirt with the Incredible Hulk on it. I'll call you after work tomorrow. Goodnight Billy, I had a great time."

She closed the door and Billy watched her as she went up the front steps and into her house. Billy backed out of the driveway, he was feeling euphoric. As he put the car into drive he thought, my yellow Hulk shirt, man I loved that shirt.

Mr. Rule passed away two weeks later. June was by Billy's side throughout his grieving. Billy and June got married three years later. They bought a big old Victorian just up from the park in Pine Tree. Wyatt was born a year after that. At the time they had no idea that he would make them stronger than they ever thought they could be.

CHAPTER FOUR

ELVIS

Elvis laid in the back of Janet Cobbler's classic 1974 International Scout. Listening to the rain which was coming down hard now. He was feeling really sad. In fact, he had not been himself all week. Elvis had a very keen sense of things, something was up.

He knew exactly where he was. He had recognized the sound of the long gravel road leading up to the training facility. Janet had been taking him here for as long as he could remember. Usually, Elvis loved it, the people were all very nice and he got to see many of his brothers and sisters. Elvis was a proud Goldador, his father had been a Golden Retriever and his mother was a Yellow Labrador.

He had 8 brothers and sisters who were all to be trained as service dogs. Each litter had a theme for its names. He was in the rock star litter. Along with Elvis was, Ozzy Osbourne, Jimi Hendrix, Janis Joplin, Kurt Cobain, Lita Ford, Billy Joel, Pat Benatar, and Axl Rose.

Elvis could hear Janet coming back now. She popped open the rear windshield and lowered the large tailgate.

"Come on Elvis, unload," Janet said.

Elvis knew this was the command to jump out of the vehicle, just as "load" was the command to jump in. Elvis jumped out into the rain and Janet snapped his leash onto his collar. She walked Elvis quickly up the steps and onto the huge covered front porch of the training facility. The building was once part of an Adirondack Great Camp. The Great Camps were built in the Adirondack Mts of N.Y. by the social elite in the late 1800s. They were used as private summer retreats. Many of the camps had fallen into ruin over time. In recent years some of the camps had been revitalized. This one, in particular, had been renovated and all the buildings were donated to different non-profit organizations.

Janet entered the building and walked Elvis into the main office. Something was definitely up, Elvis thought. They always went directly to the training gym. He had not seen any of his brothers or sisters but he had caught their scent. Janet was talking to Suzanne who ran the facility.

Suzanne said, "You can say your goodbyes out in the hall. Then one of the trainers will take him down to the gym."

Janet asked, "How long before I can visit him?"

Suzanne smiled, "That depends on how his training goes. Everyone does it a little differently. But we find it best if they don't see their foster parents for a while. I know the first time you foster is always the toughest."

Suzanne looked down at Elvis,

"Elvis sit, Elvis, stay",

She took a treat out of her fanny pack. She placed it a few feet in front of Elvis. Suzanne then said,

"Elvis leave it."

Elvis did not budge. Suzanne then picked up the treat from the floor and said,

"Yes, Elvis",

as she handed him a treat from a second fanny pack on her waist. She looked at Janet.

"He is coming along nicely, such a smart pup, I can see why you're so attached, Elvis is a real heartbreaker. I'll be in touch, we have a new litter coming soon. You did such a great job with Elvis that we would love to have you keep fostering."

Janet smiled but was thinking there was no way she could keep giving these dogs up. Suzanne had been doing this a long time and could tell Janet was uneasy about the idea.

"Janet, I know how you feel. But when you see what a difference a dog like Elvis can make in someone's life, you will see that it's all worth it."

Janet replied, "I will think about it, definitely keep me in mind."

She took Elvis out into the hall to say goodbye. Janet knelt down next to Elvis, she felt a little ridiculous as she fought back tears. She had Elvis since he was 2 months old and now he was such a big boy at 12 months.

"You're a good boy, Elvis, I know you'll make a great service dog for someone. Keep up the good work, and soon you will get to pick a forever home. I love you, buddy, I will see you again.

She gave him a few more good pets and handed him off to one of the trainers who was standing by.

Janet went back outside, it was still pouring rain out. As she crossed the deck, she looked down at her Scout and realized that she had never closed the tailgate. She ran down, closed up the back, and jumped in the truck. She sat there for a minute soaking wet, wiped away a few tears, and started to laugh. She said out loud to herself,

"Well, not too many people can say they broke up with Elvis."

Janet started to feel better as she drove away. Suzanne was right, Elvis was going to make a big difference to someone who needed him much more than she did. Janet Cobbler would most definitely foster a dog again.

Elvis was still trying to process what just happened with Janet, as Big Mike walked him down to the gym. Big Mike walked with a limp. He was a combat veteran who was wounded in Afghanistan. Elvis had worked with him a lot and liked him. Big Mike was talking to Elvis as they walked.

"Alright Elvis, this is it, you're in the show now brother. Four more months of intense training and then you'll start the matching process. You got this man, you were born for this. Besides, it could be worse, at the end of my intense training I got shot at."

When they entered the gym Elvis saw most of his brothers and sisters. He did not see or smell Pat, or Axl.

Big Mike and Elvis were still standing by the door when Suzanne walked in. She looked at them and said,

"Mike, we are gonna get the dogs up onto their tables. I want to have a few words with everyone and then we'll groom them as needed and get started."

"Sounds good," Big Mike replied, he looked down at Elvis and said "Elvis heel."

Elvis stood at attention on Big Mike's left side. Big Mike said, "Yes" and gave Elvis a small treat from a bag in his pocket. Then he said,

"Elvis, let's go", and walked Elvis across the gym to a small table that was about 3' off the ground. He looked down at Elvis and gave the command,

"Jump on".

Elvis jumped up onto the table. Big Mike gave praise,

"Yes, good job Elvis", he handed him another small treat. "You got this down already. You are gonna do just fine, man."

Suzanne gathered all the volunteers around the trainers and the dogs who were atop the grooming tables. The team was quite large. A lot of work went into the training of these dogs. Suzanne began to speak.

"Welcome everyone, as some of you already know we are going to be doing things a little differently this session.

This, our Rockstar litter will be our first group to be trained to assist those with autism. It's going to be new for all of us, including me. Some of the trainers and I have been visiting and gathering information from facilities that already do this sort of training. From what we've seen and learned this is going to take some out-of-the-box thinking. All of our clients over the years have had very unique aspects to their individual disabilities. However, this client base brings a whole new level of uniqueness. So with that, we are going to have to bring a new level of patience, and understanding, especially when we start to train with our new clients. Depending on the level of disability we will be training caregivers to be handlers as well as the clients themselves. As you can see we are starting with 7 dogs.

Axl and Pat, unfortunately, did not make the cut. They have already been adopted into loving homes. So thank you all for being here and let's make this group our best yet."

Everyone applauded and then got back to work. Big Mike started to give Elvis a once over checking his paws, teeth, and ears, he could tell that Elvis was not himself.

"What's up Buddy? You think you might want to trade places with Axl, or Pat?"

Elvis thought to himself, yup that's exactly what I was thinking. It was not fair, how come they got to go home? While he was stuck here. When all he wanted was to be with Janet. Big Mike was still talking but Elvis could not even hear him, he was so mad. How did Pat fail out? Axl, he could understand he was always up to something, too cool for school, that guy. But Pat? She was one of the best. None of this made sense.

"Hey man, I'm talking to you."

Elvis heard Big Mike say to him.

"You need to focus, you are here for a reason. This is where you are supposed to be. So stop feeling sorry for yourself. Hell, this is the Rockstar group and you're Elvis, The King of Rock-n-Roll."

Sam, one of the other trainers, was at the next table grooming Jimi. He could hear what Big Mike was telling Elvis. Sam made eye contact with Big Mike and said,

"Jimi here might have something to say about that."

Big Mike and Sam both started to laugh.

"Oh, okay see we got a challenge now. Alright, alright, The King takes on all challengers. Isn't that right Elvis?" Big Mike said with a smile.

Big Mike was right, Elvis thought. This is where he belonged. It was time to focus and finish this out. There was no turning back. He was going to make everyone proud. Now if he only knew what autism was? Oh well, he thought, I guess that would just be the next piece of the puzzle.

CHAPTER FIVE

Knowledge, Guidance, and Strength

Billy looked at the clock, 1:30 a.m., it was 30 minutes into June's shift with Wyatt, but he couldn't bring himself to wake her. Besides he might wake up Wyatt if he moved at all. He had finally fallen asleep sitting with Billy in the recliner. They had slept like this when Wyatt was a toddler, but now that he was going on 10, it was a lot less comfortable. There was an "Ice Road Truckers" marathon on. For some reason that show always seemed to help calm Wyatt. The first year after they had brought Wyatt home from the hospital he didn't sleep much at all. Billy and June would both stay up all night and then go to work in the morning when June's mom would come over. They were walking zombies and something needed to change. They decided to split up the time into shifts so they would get some sleep. The first was 9 to 1, then 1 to 5. Wyatt would never sleep more than 2 hours straight and never past 5 a.m. Even with this, Billy and June would only get 2 or 3 broken hours of rest.

Wyatt did a little better once he had been put on medicine for acid reflux. While he still never slept more than a few hours every night, he was more relaxed and didn't seem to be in pain which was a big relief.

Sitting here now Billy was thinking about when they had

taken Wyatt to the specialist who had diagnosed him with reflux. Out of nowhere during the exam, she leaned over and gave Wyatt a big kiss on his forehead. She immediately apologized, but neither Billy nor June had cared. This seemed to be a recurring theme over the years with all people that came in contact with Wyatt. He was a beautiful child with striking blue eyes, but this was not the only reason. Wyatt had an aura, or energy around him that people were drawn to, he was unique.

June had been concerned early on that Wyatt was not meeting some of his milestones. She had read an article that discussed early warning signs of autism. Wyatt seemed to display some of these signs. He would walk on his toes, stare at the ceiling fan and flap his hands. He seemed very sensitive to light, especially fluorescent light. He would be happy one minute and in extreme turmoil the next. He rarely seemed relaxed and slept very little. June did not hesitate to reach out for help. By the time Wyatt was 18 months, he had started early intervention programs. So when the official diagnosis of autism came when he turned 2, it was not a shock. Billy and June had decided early on that getting Wyatt help was much more important than any social stigma attached to having a child with autism. This would seem a simple concept, but unfortunately, there were far too many people who worried about what others would think while their child suffered.

It was hard to believe that Wyatt was 10 years old. He had been through so much already. So many different doctors, therapists, and programs. Wyatt was mostly non-verbal and would have terrible meltdowns (sensory overloads) that seemed to come out of thin air. Billy and June had eventually figured out that Wyatt was experiencing intense headaches triggered by food allergies and barometric pressure. With the help of a neurologist, they were able to treat these headaches. Wyatt would still have meltdowns but not nearly as often.

Wyatt stirred a bit and then settled again. Billy glanced at the clock, 1:47 A.M. He was actually hoping June would continue to sleep. If she got up now, Wyatt would probably wake up and not go back to sleep at all. They were a little rusty sleeping in shifts. They had only started doing it again because Wyatt was staying up most of the night the past 2 weeks. In recent years, Wyatt had been sleeping a little better although he would get up once or twice every night and still never slept past 5 A.M. Tonight, he was finally just completely exhausted.

It had been an eventful day. The security latch atop the basement door had been opened for a delivery the night before. Billy and June were more fatigued than usual and had forgotten to check it. That morning June could hear Wyatt swinging on his therapy swing as she put some laundry on. She had only been out of the room for a few minutes. When she came back the basement door was open and Wyatt was gone. June felt sick to her stomach.

She ran out the door into the backyard, yelling,

"WYATT! WYATT!"

It was just a reflex to call out. Wyatt would not have answered her if he had been there. She ran to the front of the house, but he was nowhere in sight. June got her cell phone and called the Pine Tree police, then she called Billy.

"What's up June?"

"Wyatt went out the basement door, I can't find him."

"What, how long has he been gone?"

"Not long, a few minutes maybe, I called the police already."

"OK, I'm leaving work now, I'll call Jack. He should be home and he could help look. Stay by the house in case he's hiding. Call the police back and tell them to check the park first, he may have gone there. It's going to be alright June, we'll find him."

Billy hung up, he was trying to be calm on the phone, but he was terrified. Wyatt was very vulnerable; anything could happen to him. Billy felt helpless, as he did many times over the years with Wyatt. It was often difficult to figure out how to help him. He had held Wyatt more times than he'd like to remember while he was in the throes of an uncontrollable meltdown. Billy would say over and over to Wyatt, you're alright, you're alright. Sometimes he thought he was saying it to reassure himself as much as Wyatt. He was saying it now as he raced back towards home, "You're alright, You're alright. Come on, please be alright."

◆ ◆ ◆

Wyatt had been swinging on his swing in the basement, the movement helped relax him. Sometimes he did it just for fun. Other times he did it when he felt the struggle coming on. When he was little, it seemed to happen to him almost every day. He had no control over it. He still didn't, but sometimes now he could ward it off before it got him. He had heard his mom and dad say many times over the years, "He's starting to struggle," just before he completely lost it. He could feel it coming on now, it was as if all his senses started to intensify. He had not felt it quite like this in a long time. Wyatt needed to escape. He ran to the basement door and, to his surprise, it opened. The sunlight was blinding, but he needed to keep moving. He ran up the stairs and sprinted towards the street. The noise was starting now, it would start low then build like a jet engine in his head. Wyatt put his hands over his ears as he ran down the street. He had to keep going, maybe he could outrun it this time. Tunnel vision was setting in. Wyatt could feel intense pins and needles in his hands. He took them away from his ears and started to flap them faster and faster to get rid of the sensation. The struggle was coming, he could feel the pain starting very dull in his left ear. He knew where he needed to go. Wyatt was saying, "green grass" as he ran. This sometimes helped him to calm down as he would visualize the park, his favorite place. He could barely hear himself talking now. Wyatt was focused on the park entrance, he did not see the car approaching. He sprinted across the street right in front of it. The driver screeched to a halt just in time.

"Green grass, green grass, green grass."

He was almost there but the struggle was starting to take hold. The pain in his ear was intense now and moving deeper. He ran past the swings. They would not help him at this point he needed to get to the water. Wyatt had found over the years that water could help him like nothing else. If he could just submerge himself, the water would fill his ears, block the noise and soothe his senses. But it was fall and the pool would be locked. The pond would have to do. Wyatt started to strip his clothes off. He could no longer bear the intense itching. It would not be long now, he would soon lose all control. The struggle had him in its grasp. The pain was moving to the bridge of his nose, shortly his whole head would feel like it was going to explode. Wyatt could see the pond now a few hundred yards away, he couldn't hear himself yelling, "YOU'RE ALRIGHT! YOU'RE ALRIGHT!," as he ran.

It was Saturday morning, Jack Connors was eating breakfast in his kitchen when his cell phone began to ring, it was Billy.

"What's up Billy, I thought you were working."

"Jack I need you to get over to the park, Wyatt ran away, he might have gone there."

"Shit, I'm leaving right now".

Jack just threw on his sneakers and ran out of the house in his old pajamas. There was a trail across from his house that wrapped around the pond to the main field in the park. Jack had remembered talking to Billy before about this exact thing. It was one of his biggest fears, that Wyatt would runoff. Autistic people especially children would often elope. The leading cause of death for people with autism was accidents. Many were drawn to water where they would drown. Jack knew this so he closely scanned the pond as he ran around it towards the park. Wyatt could swim, but the water temperatures this time of year could be in the 40s and no one could last long in those temps. As Jack rounded the last turn that led into the park, he saw Wyatt naked on the ground maybe a hundred feet from the water. Jack broke into an all-out sprint. As he got closer he could see that Wyatt was full-on punching himself in the forehead. Jack started to yell as he ran toward Wyatt,

"Don't do that Wyatt, you're alright."

Jack got to Wyatt and stopped him from hitting himself. Wyatt was hyperventilating. Jack was telling him everything was alright now. He realized he must have dropped his phone somewhere. Jack scooped Wyatt up and started to walk towards Billy's house. Wyatt was still struggling, but not as bad. Jack could see Pine Tree Police cruisers in the parking lot and then he saw one of the officers up ahead.

Jack yelled to him, "I got him,"

Wyatt put his hands over his ears. Jack said,

"I'm sorry buddy, I won't yell again."

When Jack reached the police, he asked them to call June. He told them that he was Wyatt's Uncle and that he was just going to keep walking toward Wyatt's house since he was starting to calm down. One of the officers gave Jack a blanket to wrap around Wyatt. As Jack neared the entrance of the park, June pulled up and jumped out of her car. She had her cell phone in her hand. Jack could hear her talking to Billy then she hung up.

"Oh my God, thank you, Jack! I'm so sorry Wyatt."

"He's okay June," said Jack as he brought Wyatt over to June's car and loaded him into the back seat.

Wyatt was smiling now. One of the officers walked up and handed June a bag with Wyatt's clothes. June thanked him, she was still crying a little. She said to Wyatt,

"You never leave the house by yourself, you know that. You scared everybody Wyatt, you can't go out by yourself, it's very dangerous."

Wyatt looked at June and said," Shake, shake, shake."

Jack said, "What's he saying?"

"He's saying, shake, he wants to go get a milkshake,"

June said as she wiped some tears away and started to laugh a little.

Jack started to laugh, "Well I guess he's over that, let's go get a shake. Give me the keys, I'll drive."

June handed him the keys and replied,

"I'll call Billy and ask him if wants one. We just go through the drive-thru."

"That's good since I'm in my PJs and Wyatt is wearing a blanket."

They all laughed at that, including Wyatt. June thought to herself, we need to figure something out. Wyatt was becoming more independent and mobile all the time. He was also getting faster as they were growing older. They needed some help, an extra set of eyes.

◆ ◆ ◆

The clock read 3:03 A.M., Billy must have dozed off. Wyatt was still sound asleep and the house was quiet. Billy carefully stretched his arm out and grabbed a blanket out of the wicker basket next to the recliner. He put it over him and Wyatt. Then he closed his eyes, thought hard, and said a prayer for Wyatt. Next, he prayed for the same three things he had always ended his prayers with. He prayed for knowledge, guidance, and strength.

Knowledge to help his friends and family. Guidance to use that knowledge. Strength, both physical and mental to carry through with whatever he needed to do. Billy could not remember when or why he had started praying for these three things, he just always had. He whispered it again,

"Knowledge, guidance, and strength."

His eyes grew heavy and he fell into a deep sleep for the first time in years.

"Billy, Billy, wake up."

June said as she stood over Billy who was still lying in the recliner. Billy abruptly woke up,

"What time is it, Where's Wyatt?"

"He's fine, he's upstairs taking a bath. My mom is watching him. It's 7:15 A.M. I am taking him horseback riding soon."

Wyatt went to equine therapy on Sunday mornings.

"Wow, I really passed out, what time did he get up?"

"I just came down and got him from you about 20 minutes ago, he's never slept that late. I guess his little adventure took a lot out of him. I've been thinking about that all night and doing some research. I want to look into getting Wyatt a service dog."

"Okay, when did you come up with that idea?"

"It was weird, I sprung awake at 3:09 A.M., and had this idea that a service dog would be the perfect thing for Wyatt. So I started to research it."

Billy started to get out of the recliner slowly, he was stiff as hell from sleeping in it all night.

"Sounds like a great idea, 3:09 you say, that was a quick answer," Billy said, making a little joke to himself.

June ignored him. She was eager to talk more about the service dog.

"There's a place just north of Lake Placid that is currently training autism service dogs. I filled out an application for Wyatt."

"That would be awesome! I think a dog would be good for Wyatt." Billy said with a smile.

He had a good feeling about this Idea. "That's exactly what Wyatt needs.

CHAPTER SIX

A Boy and His Dog

A woman's voice that he didn't recognize was saying, "Good job, Elvis, stay with your boy."

Elvis was jogging next to a boy. The boy stopped running. Elvis stopped and sat. The boy knelt on one knee and started to pet Elvis. He still did not know who the boy was but he felt a warm closeness to him. The boy did not say anything, just smiled and laughed. The lady was there now too.

"Good boy Elvis," she said.

Elvis was happy, the boy started to jog again. Elvis followed alongside him. It was a beautiful day. He could see endless fields of green grass.

Elvis woke up suddenly, he was in his crate at the training facility. He let out a short sigh, the dream had seemed so real. Elvis gazed up at the big clock on the wall, 3:09 A.M. It would be another couple of hours before anyone would let him out of his crate. Elvis could not fall back asleep. He had a strong sense now that his forever home was out there. He just had to be patient for a little longer. It would all work out.

Later that morning, Elvis was walking with Big Mike on one of the campus trails doing some off-leash training. Big Mike had Elvis lay down next to a big Locust tree log that had been turned into a bench. Then he sat down himself.

"Let's take a little break here for a minute, Elvis."

It was very quiet, just a few distant birds chirping. Big Mike was staring off into space. Elvis could tell that he was somewhere else at the moment, deep in thought. He had seen Big Mike do this before, he would drift off. Elvis could sense Big Mike's heart rate elevating when he was like this, he did not like it. Big Mike was deep in this time, his foot began to tap rapidly and he clenched his fists. Elvis groaned and jumped up with his front paws on Big Mike's lap. Big Mike snapped out of it.

"Good boy, Elvis. It's alright, thank you."

He was petting Elvis with both hands. Elvis could sense Big Mike's heart starting to normalize now.

"Sorry about that Elvis, every time I think I got that shit beat, it tries to get me. The darkness is a sneaky mother. Don't worry, I'm stronger than it."

Big Mike started to laugh. He stood up, patted Elvis on the head, and snapped his leash back on. They started a slow walk back towards the training facility. Big Mike started to talk to Elvis.

"Won't be long now Elvis, you've done a great job these last four months. In the next few weeks, clients will start coming in. Remember you pick your family. You're the one with all the sense, you'll know when the match is right."

Elvis was listening to Big Mike, he wished he could tell him about his dream. His family was out there already. But it would be a miracle if they found each other. Then, almost on cue, Big Mike said,

"You have to have faith, they'll come."

Billy was in the driver's seat, and Wyatt was buckled up on the back passenger's side. They were waiting in the driveway for June to come out. It would be their third attempt at going to meet some of the service dogs. The first time there was a last-minute cancellation by the facility, which completely turned June off on the whole place. How could a facility that was providing services for people with autism cancel at the last minute? It would have been different if it had been an emergency, but it seemed as if it were just a scheduling conflict; June had been furious. Wyatt had been in the car ready to go. Billy understood why June was upset. However, he pointed out that making too big a deal of it this early in the process would be cutting their noses off to spite their face. June calmed down and agreed to let it go, but momma bear was definitely not happy. It reeked of a lack of understanding for the client base it was supposedly serving.

The second time Wyatt had been having a bad few days. He wasn't sleeping and his anxiety was elevated. About halfway up to the training facility, Wyatt started to struggle. They had no choice but to turn back. From past experience, Billy and June knew there was no way Wyatt would get through the rest of the trip. They'd only be getting further from home, destined to fail. So they turned back. June called the facility to let them know the situation. Billy could hear the girl on the other end tell June,

"Well, I guess we're even."

Billy thought to himself, Oh boy, strike two, but if it bothered June she didn't let on. She just made another appointment.

June came out of the house and got in the front passenger's seat and they were on their way. Wyatt was in good spirits, his normal silly self. Billy was doing his best to put on a good face. Inside he was anxious, he often was when they took Wyatt to new places. He tried to fight back these feelings because he believed Wyatt could pick up on his stress as Wyatt was super sensitive to all his surroundings. Simply put, Wyatt was like a computer that was always downloading everything in his environment. Other people's emotions, weather changes, noises, colors, numbers, shapes, on and on; a continuous flow with no ability to filter. Sometimes it became too much and that computer would crash. Billy was always anticipating the crash, dreading it. Trying to figure out ways to head it off. There could be a fine line between helping Wyatt and inhibiting him. Billy was careful not to let his insecurities take away from Wyatt's experiences. One of many things he had learned when raising a child with autism, personal insecurities were a roadblock more than ever.

New Clients had started to come to the training facility to meet Elvis and the other dogs. In the beginning stages, Suzanne would have clients come in and meet all the dogs. Many times the dogs would gravitate towards someone. In essence, the dog picked the client, not the other way around and she found this made for the quickest and best bonds. She would also rotate the dogs between the clients and keep a watchful eye on their interactions as a good initial bond was critical. Most of the dogs had been matched with clients in recent weeks, only Elvis and Ozzy had remained.

Elvis had liked all the people that he had been introduced to, but he had not gotten the vibe off them, that he had gotten off the boy in his dream. Elvis had been acting a little standoffish with the clients because he did not want to be matched. He was starting to think that maybe he should loosen up a little. After all, he was basing everything on his dream. He could tell that Suzanne was beginning to get a little annoyed with him. Big Mike on the other hand would yes Suzanne to death but had still shown Elvis support when she was not around. He would tell Elvis not to worry that he would know when it was right.

Big Mike was having his morning coffee in the break room. He had put Elvis in a down-stay under the table. The dogs were trained to lie under a table so that they would be out of the way in a restaurant or other similar public places. Suzanne came in and told Big Mike that they had two clients coming in that day. A teenage girl that morning and a young boy in the afternoon. Elvis was listening and his ears perked up when he had heard her mention the boy. Suzanne continued,

"The young lady's name is Krystal, she has severe autism. Her mom told me that she does not do well in large indoor spaces. So we are going to meet here this morning. Sarah will be bringing in Ozzy so have Elvis ready as well. The family should arrive in about a half-hour thanks Mike," Suzanne left the room.

Big Mike started to talk to Elvis,

"Alright man you heard her, two clients today. I've been telling you to be patient but we are getting down to crunch time now. So step up your game and be a little more open-minded." Elvis was listening and agreed.

Elvis and Ozzy were laying down next to each other in the farthest corner of the breakroom from the door. Big Mike and Sarah were sitting on opposite sides of them. Suzanne came in with Krystal and her parents. Krystal was wearing a gray hoodie with the hood pulled down hiding her face. She seemed nervous and timid.

Her mom said,

"Krystal, why don't you sit down over here."

She directed her to a chair near the door. Krystal sat down. She was wringing her hands together nonstop. Suzanne said softly,

"Would you like to meet one of the dogs, Krystal ?"

She did not respond. Krystal's mom knelt down next to her and whispered in her ear. Then she said to Suzanne,

"Why don't we just bring one of the dogs over and see what happens?"

Suzanne agreed and asked Big Mike to bring Elvis over off-leash. Elvis approached Krystal, she was now rubbing her hands on the top of her thighs.

Suzanne said,

"This is Elvis, Krystal, do you want to pet him?"

Elvis was putting out his best chill vibe, he was trying to let Krystal know that everything was going to be okay. Elvis leaned in a little closer.

Krystal yelled, "NO",

and swatted Elvis on the nose. Big Mike said,

"Whoa, back Elvis, back."

He had Elvis back off and lay down. Elvis was not hurt just a little in shock. She did not hit him very hard. Krystal's mom told her,

"You do not hit."

She apologized to everyone and said that Krystal was usually very gentle, but she struggled in new environments and was having an especially tough time as of late. Krystal started to rock back and forth. She then began to sob and say,

"I'm sorry, I'm sorry", over and over again.

Krystal's dad started to rub her back as her mom whispered to her again. Elvis felt terrible for her. At that moment and without any commands, Ozzy went over to Krystal and put his head right on her lap. Krystal began to pet him, she slid onto the floor. Ozzy laid down next to her and she continued to pet him. She was no longer crying, in fact, she was starting to smile. Ozzy had found his match.

Billy, June, and Wyatt had arrived at the training facility about 30 minutes early. It was always tricky trying to plan out arrival times for appointments. They usually tried to arrive 5 or 10 minutes before with the hope that they could get Wyatt right in. The longer the trip, the harder that was to do. Because Wyatt was so deeply connected to his environment his mood could be hard to predict especially on trips. Billy parked out front of the main building and June ran inside to check things out. Billy sometimes joked that bringing Wyatt places was like providing security for a dignitary. The truth was it did help to scope things out prior to

Wyatt going, so they could avoid any possible pitfalls or triggers. Sometimes they would even take pictures ahead of time and create a social story for Wyatt. A social story was a short story with pictures. It helped an autistic person become familiar with a new place before going. Simple but detailed: first, you will walk up these stairs, second you will go through this door, and third, you will see this person. Wyatt was very visual as many people with autism are so it helped a great deal to have pictures to go along with verbal descriptions.

As they sat and waited for June to come back out, Billy was telling Wyatt about the facility and the dogs. Wyatt was very quiet and Billy could see that he had his finger in his ear. This was not a good sign, he could be starting to struggle. Billy saw June come back out, he got out of the car to talk to her.

June said,

"They are ready now, we can bring him in."

As he walked around to the passengers' side Billy replied,

"He seems very quiet and has his finger in his ear, not sure he's ready."

June opened Wyatt's door,

"Come on Wyatt, do you want to go in and meet the dogs?"

Wyatt put a finger in each ear, hunched over, and squinted his eyes shut.

"Alright buddy take a minute and relax, then we'll go in," June said.

As the parent of a child with autism, there were many things Billy and June had to navigate differently. Wyatt could just be misbehaving as any child would. In these instances, you could use your parenting 101 handbooks. In a situation like this, he was obviously experiencing some physical or mental pain or both. Discipline would be useless, he needed help. Sometimes it was as simple as patience and time so he could work through whatever was troubling him. The handbook might tell you to give Wyatt a stern warning or a smack on the butt. Billy and June had heard all the ignorance before, including the tough-guy stance. "I'd pull that little bastard right out of the car, he'd listen then." This would result in a full-on meltdown. Wyatt would more than likely wind up on the ground flailing around to the point of throwing up. While trying to bang his head or punch himself as hard as he could. The ignorant would scramble through their parenting handbook for their next brilliant move and come up empty. Because the behavior had nothing to do with defiance. It was the end result of built-up anguish. In a person who had a difficult time expressing their distress before it was too late.

Billy stayed with Wyatt as June went back in to tell Suzanne the situation. Suzanne was in the gym with Big Mike, Elvis, and some of the other trainers. June told Suzanne that Wyatt was having a little bit of a tough time at the moment, but that they were still going to try and get him to come in. Big Mike was listening and before Suzanne could say anything he said,

"Well I could take Elvis out to see Wyatt. He's super chill, maybe he could help?"

"That would be great, it might help if he could see one of the dogs."

Suzanne said, "That would be fine, we are trying to think outside the box with this group."

Big Mike looked at June and said, "Lead the way, Elvis and I will follow."

Suzanne stayed back as they made their way out to the front of the building. June said to Big Mike,

"Thanks for doing this."

Big Mike said,

"We are trying to think outside the box with this group,"

In his best Suzanne impression.

Then he smiled and said,

"It's no trouble that's why we're here, don't mind Suzanne either. She's a great trainer, but very structured. She reminds me of a few drill Sergeants I had. She means well though."

June laughed as they entered the lobby. She said,

"Sorry I didn't get your name?"

Big Mike smiled, "Oh that's my fault, I was in too big a hurry to escape Suzanne before she changed her mind. I'm Mike, people call me Big Mike. And this is Elvis."

Big Mike had Elvis sit to greet June.

"You could pet him now if you want before we go out."

June smiled again and said,

"I'm June and my husband Billy is outside with my son Wyatt, he's ten."

She then bent down to greet Elvis.

Elvis had a strange feeling come over him. He felt like he needed to do something but he didn't know what. Then he saw the woman come into the gym and begin talking to Suzanne. He knew her but from where? As they walked down the hall it came to him this might be the woman from his dream. She bent down and said,

"Hello Elvis, good boy. Would you like to meet my son Wyatt?"

Elvis knew this was the woman from his dream.

June walked out onto the front porch followed by Big Mike and Elvis. She heard Billy say,

"Over here",

He was standing down at the far corner of the giant covered porch. Wyatt was sitting on a bench in front of him. They made their way down to Billy and Wyatt. June asked,

"How's he doing?"

Billy said, "Well I got him out of the car but when we got onto the porch he ran down here and sat. He's definitely busy and saying something under his breath over and over."

June introduced Billy to Big Mike and Elvis. She then sat next to Wyatt and said,

"Yeah I can hear him saying something very fast I can't make it out."

Elvis was sitting at Big Mike's side, trying to remain extremely chill, but he was very excited. He could not believe it, this was definitely his boy. Elvis could hear Wyatt saying "green grass," very fast with each breath. He could sense the boy was deep inside himself and not aware of his surroundings. He wanted to go to him as Ozzy had with Krystal, however, he didn't want to rush anything so he decided to wait.

Big Mike said,

"How about I bring Elvis a little closer and introduce him to Wyatt."

Billy and June agreed that would be a good idea. Big Mike brought Elvis over and had him sit in front of Wyatt. Wyatt had his hands cupped over his ears as he slowly rocked back and forth. Elvis could tell the boy was now conscious of what was going on. He was no longer saying anything. The boy leaned forward, eye to eye with Elvis. Their foreheads almost touched. Elvis had that warm feeling, he could sense the boy was calm now. The boy gently put his hands over Elvis's ears, leaned a little further forward, and rested his forehead against Elvis's. The boy did not say a word but Elvis got a vibe he could almost hear in his head,

"Hello Elvis, I'm Wyatt. Nice to meet you."

Elvis sent the vibe back, "Hello Wyatt, nice to finally meet you."

Wyatt smiled and laughed. Elvis was not sure if that just happened or if he had imagined it. One thing was certain he definitely felt a connection to this boy named Wyatt.

Billy, June, and Big Mike had been watching somewhat in amazement. June was fighting back tears.

"Is this what usually happens?"

Big Mike shook his head,

"I thought the meeting we had this morning with another client was amazing, but it doesn't get any better than this. Not to jinx anything this early, but I'd say Elvis has found his match."

Big Mike could see Suzanne leaning out the front door looking down at them, he gave her a thumbs up.

June started her training a week later to be Elvis's main handler. Wyatt went a few times too and even learned some basic commands. Elvis was trained to be mainly off leash with Wyatt. He would stay by his side and even corral him away from danger if Wyatt bolted unexpectedly. He added, heightened visibility and made others more aware of Wyatt. He helped with Wyatt's anxiety and was a loyal friend and companion. Elvis had found his forever home.

CHAPTER SEVEN

WATCH OUT WYATT!!

Billy took off early from work to go and talk to Tim Houzer about Wyatt being part of the football team. Aside from being the Eighth-grade football coach, Tim was also a PE teacher at Pine Tree H.S. Billy could see a large truck crane lifting some of the new stadium lights into place as he pulled into the high school parking lot. He recognized Tim standing alongside another man who also looked familiar. They were standing on the outdoor basketball court having a conversation. Billy got out of his van and made his way over. As he got closer both men said,

"Hey, Billy."

The shorter man with Tim stepped forward and put out his hand.

"Long time no see Billy, Frank Reilly."

Billy smiled wide, "Hey Frank, good to see you man, how have you been?"

Billy had always liked and admired Frank. He had taken a lot of unwarranted criticism after missing that field goal against Walnut Heights. But he never let it bother him. At least he never showed that it did. He would just laugh it off. Billy remembered a few months after Frank's miss. Scott Norwood would miss his infamous field goal in the Superbowl. Frank went out and bought a Norwood jersey and wore it around town. He turned the whole thing into a joke. Billy had always thought that was a great way to handle the situation.

"I'm good Billy, I just moved back to the area, I'm going to be helping Tim out with the team. He was telling me about Wyatt. My nephew is autistic, so if there's anything I can do to help out let me know."

"I appreciate that Frank, thanks," Billy said as he shook hands with Tim.

Tim said, "Do you want to talk here? Or we could go inside to my office?"

"No, here's fine, this shouldn't take long. You might as well hear this too, Frank, since you're going to be helping out. So I guess the idea would be to have Wyatt around the team for practices and maybe go to some of the games. We have already arranged for a 1:1 aide to be with him. She's also trained to handle his service dog, Elvis. Wyatt ranges from moderate to severe on the autism spectrum. He does communicate using one or two-word phrases but he's mostly nonverbal, especially in new settings. He is however very active and athletic when he's able to focus. We are open to suggestions, mainly we just want him to be able to interact with his peers as much as possible. If you guys think it won't work out, or if a problem arises please don't hesitate to let us know."

Tim said, "No problem Billy, I'm actually familiar with Wyatt. My wife Debra was an aide in his elementary school class. I think it will work out fine. I've been thinking about it already. Tony Connors had mentioned it to me a while back. We could have him do some of the stretching and calisthenics. Then maybe have him pair off with the kickers. Tony mentioned that he liked to kick, we'll work it out. I also know his 1:1, Molly McNeil."

"Great, I should have known Anthony would be out ahead of this. Just so you know it's not so much that Wyatt likes to kick, but that Anthony would like him to kick. He has it in his head that Wyatt will be good at it. And yes Molly is Wyatts 1:1, she is great with him. I remember Debra, but I didn't know she was your wife."

Frank interjected, "Anthony, that's Jack's son Tony?"

"Oh yeah, we still call him Anthony but all the kids and teachers call him Tony now," said Billy.

Frank laughed, "Yeah my family still calls me Franklyn, but no one else ever did."

"I didn't even know your name was Franklyn," said Billy.

"That was the point, pretty sure you clowns would have some-how busted my chops about it," Frank said with a smile.

Billy replied, "I don't know about that, maybe if the turtle had been around then. Hey, come to think of it…wasn't that one of the books? " Franklyn hooks left," about him missing a field goal."

They all laughed,

"Wow, you had to go there," said Tim.

Billy was still smiling,

"Frank knows I'm kidding, that's ancient history."

"Yeah I just missed a field goal, it's not like I fell down with an open field ahead of me."

Billy cracked up, "Those are fighting words, Franklyn."

Frank smiled again, "Seriously though Billy, maybe I can help Wyatt to kick. I know a bunch of different drills and stuff. We can make it fun for him while still getting our work in."

Billy said, "I really appreciate it guys, this is great, I hope it works out."

Tim said, "Listen if he winds up liking it, we could probably set something up with one of the other teams where he could kick in a game."

Billy shrugged a little, "I don't think that would be a good idea, Tim. That can be a nice thing for some kids. I don't think that would be best for Wyatt. He's very aware of stuff like that. I'm pretty sure he would pick up on the fact it was a setup. It would probably cause him more anxiety than anything."

Tim put his hands up, "Oh, no problem, just throwing it out there."

Billy replied, "Don't take it the wrong way, I know you're just trying to help. It's sometimes hard to figure Wyatt out. One thing I noticed is that people underestimate him and he can use it to his advantage."

"How do you mean?" said Frank.

"They talk in front of him about things they don't necessarily want him to know, as you may do with a small child. Wyatt listens to everything and then sometimes takes advantage. I've called him out on it from time to time and he laughs. Then there are other times when he has a really difficult time focusing on simple tasks. This can change pretty quickly, something he did 5 minutes before with no effort could become difficult and vice versa. I guess that's one reason autism is represented with a puzzle piece. It can be exactly that, puzzling."

Tim nodded his head in agreement and said,

"Well I guess the first step is getting him to practice on Monday, we'll figure it out. I know a lot of the kids are excited to have Wyatt and Elvis around."

"Sounds good, we'll just take it one step at a time. Hey, I see the new stadium lights are going up. Kinda sad to see the old ones come down. But I guess it's long overdue for an update," said Billy.

"You should go over there and check it out. The new field is already in, looks like a college setup," said Tim.

"Yeah anonymous donor, you don't think it could be Glenn?" Frank said with a not-so-subtle hint of sarcasm.

"I wouldn't know, you should ask him yourself, he's moving back here full-time next week."

By the look on their faces, Billy could tell that it was not such a big secret.

"Looks like you guys already knew that."

Tim nodded, "Yeah he actually called me the other day. Asked me if I wanted to coach the Varsity team next year. Told me that his father and some of the other townspeople wanted him to coach. He didn't think that was a great idea to have him out front. Said it would draw too much unwanted attention and take away from the kids."

"Are you gonna do it?" asked Billy.

"I'm thinking about it, that's actually what I was talking to Frank about."

Frank chimed in, "What do you think Billy?"

"Well if I didn't know any better, I'd say no way. Who wants some guy looking over your shoulder. Especially Superman, the town legend, but that's not the case with Glenn. You guys know how laid back he has always been, he's even more so now. I think it would actually be a great situation if you want to do it. Glenn is really smart and he knows how to deal with people. At the same time, he's not going to override any decisions you make as a coach. I really think he just wants to help the kids."

Tim agreed, "That's pretty much what we were thinking. It would also be nice to win some games around here again. The team has had three coaches in the past five years and as many wins."

"Well I think you guys should do it then, maybe you can finally take down Walnut Heights." Billy patted Frank on the shoulder.

Frank shook his head," Those assholes won another State Championship last year. And you know who the coach is? Their old Tight End from when we played, Chuck Foster."

"What a dick that guy was," said Tim.

Billy laughed, "He's actually not a bad guy. I did some work at his house a few years ago. He's totally different now."

"He's coaching Walnut Heights, you don't get that job without being a dick," said Frank.

Billy chuckled as he shook hands with Tim and Frank.

"Yeah you're right, Frank, screw him. I'll catch you guys next week, it was great talking to you."

As Billy walked back to his van he had a good feeling about Wyatt playing with the team. He really hoped it would work out.

Tony had been made the starting center on the team. So every day at practice, he would get some work snapping the ball with the kickers. Wyatt had been coming to practice and was doing well. He had done all the stretching and was even running laps with the team, but they had no luck trying to get him to kick.

One Friday at the end of practice some of the boys were trying to get Coach Reilly to kick a field goal.

"Come on Coach, my dad said that you kicked in college," exclaimed Tony.

"That was a long time ago guys," said Coach Reilly.

"Come on Coach, let's see what you got," the boys shouted.

"Alright if I can hit one from 45 you guys have to run an extra lap, deal?"

The boys agreed, they didn't think the old man had any chance at hitting one from that distance. Little did they know that Frank Reilly was in great shape and had never stopped kicking. Wyatt had been off to the side with Molly and Elvis. Tony went over to bring him closer.

"Watch this Wyatt, Coach Reilly is going to kick."

Wyatt was smiling as he walked over to get a better view. Coach Reilly put the ball on the kicking tee and took his steps back off the ball.

He yelled, "You guys ready to run?"

With two smooth strides, his leg exploded on the ball. It flew high in the air and split the uprights. The boys were all excited and laughing. Tony looked at Wyatt, he had the biggest smile on his face.

One of the boys grabbed another ball and said,

"Double or nothing from 50."

Coach Reilly smiled, "Only if everyone wants to do it because you guys are going to run the extra laps if I hit it."

The boys all agreed to have him kick again. Wyatt moved in

even closer to watch. Tony went to pull him back a little, but Coach Reilly told him that Wyatt was fine where he was.

Wyatt had been amazed by the first kick. He loved everything about it. From the thud of the initial impact to the trajectory and distance the ball traveled.

Coach Reilly really blasted the next one. With a tremendous boom, it flew even higher in the air, easily good from fifty. Wyatt jumped up and down with a huge smile and patted Tony on the back.

"That was awesome, right Wyatt?" Tony said.

"Awesome, awesome, awesome," replied Wyatt.

One of the other boys asked,

"Why aren't you kicking in the NFL Coach Reilly?"

Coach Reilly smirked, "I'm waiting for them to change the rules, so I can kick on an open field off a tee. Alright, guys let's go over to see Coach Houzer on the track."

The boys grumbled a little as they jogged over to see Coach Houzer. Wyatt had drifted off a little in the opposite direction. Molly let Elvis off-leash and gave him a command,

"Elvis, go to your boy."

Elvis ran over to Wyatt's side and Molly followed.

Tony had lagged behind to talk to Coach Reilly.

"Hey Coach, that was great. Wyatt really liked it, I think you sparked his interest."

"Do you want to try and get him to kick a few now?" replied Coach Reilly.

"No, I don't think so. Wyatt doesn't always like to try stuff right away, especially when he likes it. Even when he got a new toy he really liked, he would wait to try it out when he thought nobody was watching. Sometimes it would take him days before he even went near it."

"That's interesting," said Coach Reilly.

"Even though he seems not to care, I think sometimes he likes to be good at stuff before he'll do it in front of other people. Then other times he'll take off his swimsuit and jump in a crowded town swimming pool, butt naked."

Coach Reilly was laughing, "So what do you think our next step is then Tony?"

"I'll try and get him to kick at the park this weekend. I could be wrong, but I have a strong feeling that Wyatt is going to want to kick now."

"Well let me know what happens. You can always call me. I would come and meet you guys at the park or even here sometimes when the field is open if you want to practice. You know you should think about working with people with disabilities. You have three great qualities, empathy, selflessness, and leadership. Those are rare commodities, especially nowadays."

"Thanks, Coach, I'd like to open a gym someday that focuses on helping people with disabilities."

"I think you should Tony."

"Yeah, we'll see, thanks again, Coach Reilly. I'll let you know how it goes with Wyatt."

Tony heard his dad yell up to him from downstairs.

"Hey Anthony, get your butt out of bed and have some breakfast. It's 8:30 already."

Anthony rolled his eyes, he had friends who laid in bed until noon on Saturday. Try telling that to his dad.

"Alright I'll be down in a minute, on second thought I'll take breakfast in bed," Tony yelled down.

"You'll take a kick in the ass, get down here," Jack replied.

Tony wandered down a few minutes later. Jack was loading dishes into the dishwasher.

"Your mom took your sister to dance lessons, what are you doing today? Are you going to the park with Wyatt? Because your Uncle Billy called and said you guys created a monster. That's all Wyatt's been saying kick, kick, kick. He's like a little Gary Anderson."

"Gary Who?" asked Tony.

"Never mind, so what's up, you going?"

"Yeah, I told Aunt June I'd meet them at 10. Wyatt has swimming first. That's great news though, is he really saying it three times?"

"That's funny I asked your Uncle the same thing. He said yes, he's saying it three times."

It didn't always hold true, but Wyatt had a habit of repeating things three times if he was interested in something. If you asked him a question especially more than once and he did not answer, that usually meant no. If you asked him and he repeated it once it was a definite maybe. However if you asked him a question and he repeated part of it back three times or said OK, OK, OK, it was a yes. This was a very positive sign. Tony could not wait to get to the park.

There was a football field in the park. Tony had arrived early to set up some cones and mark out some distances. He was not there long when he saw Wyatt and Elvis running towards him with Aunt June jogging behind.

Tony set the football up in the kicking tee holder at the 20-yard line. He figured this would be a good distance to start from. Wyatt had slowed to a walk as he got close.

"Hey Wyatt ready to do some kicking?" said Tony.

"Oh, he's ready. All he's been doing since he got home last night is watching videos on kicking field goals. I barely got him out of the house to go swimming this morning," replied June.

Wyatt gave Tony a high five and walked past him towards the ball. He circled around it like a golfer lining up a putt. He had a very serious look on his face until he noticed Tony and June watching him. He gave them a little smirk. Then like he'd been kicking his whole life he took his steps off the ball. Took two strides towards it and kicked the ball dead center through the uprights.

Tony yelled, "Holy Cow, he split the uprights! Good job Wyatt."

Wyatt had a big grin on his face.

"Did you see that, Aunt June?" Tony exclaimed as he got the ball back from Elvis.

"Yes, see if he'll do it again. I got to record it this time." June took out her phone and got a little closer.

"Alright Wyatt let's try that again," Tony placed the ball back in the holder.

Wyatt lined it up the same way and kicked it perfectly dead center. Tony backed the tee up to the 25, and Wyatt kicked 4 more from that distance with ease. Tony backed it up even further to the 30, which would be a 40-yard field goal.

"Make sure you record this one Aunt June, it's a 40-yard attempt. Go ahead Wyatt, you got this man."

Wyatt went through his motions the same way. He kicked the ball but this time it hooked left, good just inside the upright.

Tony gave Wyatt a high five,

"That's great Wyatt, unbelievable, you get that Aunt June?"

"I got it Anthony, great job Wyatt, really good Buddy," said June.

Tony retrieved the ball from Elvis and teed it back up.

"Try one more Wyatt," said Tony.

Wyatt kicked another from 40, this time he really kicked it hard. It had plenty of distance but it hooked even further left no good. Wyatt clapped his hands and shook his head in disappointment.

"That's alright Wyatt everyone misses, maybe we're a little far out. Still great for your first time actually trying."

Tony moved the ball two yards closer.

"Try from here Wyatt."

Wyatt hit a half dozen more from 38 splitting the uprights every time. The last one he kicked had much less distance on it. Tony and June agreed that it was probably time to wrap things up. With some coaxing and the promise of a milkshake, they were able to convince Wyatt of the same. They wanted him to end on a positive note.

Later that day Tony asked his dad if he could send the video of Wyatt kicking to Coach Reilly. Jack told him that Coach Reilly was a friend so it should be fine. About an hour later he got a reply.

Coach R: This is unreal Tony, has Wyatt been

practicing somewhere else?

Tony: No, he just watched a bunch of kicking

videos, came to the park and started kicking.

Coach R: His steps looked perfect every time. I saw a

couple of things we could work on with those

longer ones. But this is beyond a great start.

Good job Tony, I'll see you at practice on

Monday.

Over the next couple of weeks at practice, Wyatt was kicking the ball extremely well off the tee. He had been a little reluctant to kick once they started to have him try it with a snap and a live holder, but before long he was even kicking in practice scrimmages. All the boys were aware that they could try and block Wyatt's kicks, but not hit him. Although, Tony thought Wyatt would not have cared much. He was a year older and bigger than most of the kids on the team. Wyatt had actually liked it when they would rush him, he thought it was funny. That being said Billy was more than a little nervous when Tim and Frank had asked if Wyatt could participate in live-action practice. He agreed with the assurance that no one would tackle Wyatt. He would only kick and he would never be put into a real game.

Towards the end of the season in a practice scrimmage, Wyatt kicked a picture-perfect 50-yarder. All the kids and coaches went crazy, they could not believe it. Even Elvis barked, which he never did. Tony had not seen Wyatt laugh so hard since they were little. He appeared to really love seeing how excited everyone was. One of the boys had recorded the kick and posted it online, " Autistic boy kicks a 50-yard field goal," and the video went viral.

Billy was cleaning out his garage on a Sunday morning when his phone rang, it was Tim Houzer.

"What's up, Tim?"

"Hey Billy, not much just wanted to talk to you about Wyatt. Now I know you said you absolutely don't want him to play in a real game. But I thought you may reconsider?"

Tim was not done with his thoughts when Billy cut him off.

"Yeah, no way Tim. Wyatt is so unpredictable that he could easily get hurt. Listen, he loves to practice and the whole experience has been great, but I just see no benefit to him playing in a game. I honestly don't think it makes any difference to him. So even if there's a slim chance that he will get hurt, it's still not worth the risk."

"I hear what you're saying Billy, but I really think the chance of him getting hurt is less than slim. Even in practice the kid that's the holder knows to either run or fall on the ball when Wyatt doesn't kick or the rush comes in too fast. Wyatt is definitely unpredictable. There are still times he won't kick after the snap, but most of the time now he does. I'm not saying he's going to do it all the time. Everyone just thinks that it would be good if he could just do it once. If he kicks it great, if he doesn't, no big deal. He's never going to have the ball so he's not going to get hit."

Billy was listening to Tim and he was still not thrilled with the idea. At the same time, he was thinking of his personal insecurity rule. He did not want to inhibit Wyatt because of his own fear.

"Alright Tim let me talk it over with June and I'll get back to you."

"Sounds good Billy, enjoy the rest of your Sunday."

After discussing it with June they decided to let Wyatt try it. If Wyatt was having a good day and the opportunity presented itself, Wyatt would kick.

The last game of the year was being played at Pine Tree high school. It was a beautiful fall day and all the kids were very excited to play on the new turf field. Billy had wanted to be on the sidelines for this game. He was still nervous about Wyatt possibly getting in the game. But June had vetoed that idea. She told him that he would only make Wyatt anxious. Billy knew she was right, besides Molly and Elvis were with Wyatt.

It had been a good game but the visiting team had pulled away in the fourth quarter. With a little over two minutes left Pine Tree had the ball. It was fourth down with the ball on the 20-yard line. Tim Houzer called a time-out. Billy saw that Anthony had gone over to get Wyatt. Billy thought he might throw up. He was so nervous. June and Jack were sitting on either side of him.

They could see how worked up he was getting.

"Take a breath man, you're going to have a heart attack. Why don't you go down by the fence next to Glenn?" said Jack.

Billy had not even noticed Glenn standing next to the field holding the large Eighth-grade Championship trophy. He got up without saying a word and walked down next to Glenn.

"What's up Billy," said Glenn.

Billy smiled, "They're putting Wyatt in to kick and I think I'm going to puke. Other than that everything is good."

"There's a pretty big cup on this trophy, so if you're going to spew, spew into this," Glenn said in his best, "Garth Algar" voice.

Billy laughed for a second and then saw Wyatt going out onto the field with Anthony by his side. The crowd erupted in cheers. Billy hadn't realized how many people were aware of Wyatt.

"I'm going to get a little closer," Billy said to Glenn as he hopped over the fence.

Billy was standing on the sideline as the ball was snapped. The holder, Kenny Austin, put the ball down for Wyatt to kick it, but Wyatt froze. Anthony was blocking 3 players in a desperate attempt to give Wyatt some more time. And even though Kenny had been told multiple times to just fall on the ball he too panicked. He reverted back to his normal real game scenario. He flipped the ball back to the kicker as the defense broke through the line. Wyatt caught the ball.

Billy yelled, "Watch out Wyatt!"

But it was too late, Wyatt got blasted in the back as two other players hit him from the front. Billy was on the field before the players even got up. Elvis had broken loose from Molly and sprinted onto the field as well. Tony was pulling players off of Wyatt as Billy approached. He looked down at Wyatt who was smiling.

"Are you OK buddy? You took a pretty good hit," said Billy.

Wyatt looked at him and said, "Again, again, again."

"No, I think we are done here today, good job Wyatt. Get up slow."

Billy got Wyatt up and the crowd started to cheer. Billy could hear Anthony yelling at the other team.

"Anthony, knock it off, they did nothing wrong. It's a real game. It's my fault, nobody else's," Billy yelled.

Tim and Frank had come up to Billy to apologize. He reassured them not to worry. He reiterated that it was his fault. Billy told June on the ride home that he did not want Wyatt playing anymore, not even practice. He would eventually back off this hardline stance. Billy agreed to let Wyatt practice again. But Wyatt Rule's playing days were over.

CHAPTER EIGHT

It's Now or Never

Mike Bass had been given the nickname, "Badass", by one of his Ranger School instructors. It was meant to be sarcastic. Mike was a huge man who excelled in all the skills needed to be an Army Ranger. However, he was also the nicest, most polite person anyone had ever met. Because of his demeanor, it had been hinted that maybe Mike was too nice. Some thought he may not perform in combat. That would all change during his first tour as a Ranger in Afghanistan.

Mike's Rifle squad had been traveling in two Humvees on a narrow road in Kabul province. They had taken that route before on their way to Jalalabad and had met no resistance. Mike had always remembered hysterically laughing at the conversation going on, just before his life changed forever.

Corporal Joe Righetti, from Pelham N.Y., had been arguing with Private first class, Brian McKenna, from Lakewood Arkansas. McKenna had been of the mindset that the song, "Ice Ice Baby," by Vanilla Ice was a classic with staying power. Righetti not only hated Vanilla Ice but insisted that the song, "Informer," by Snow was a better jam that had been underrated. Mike had been trying to stay impartial, besides he had thought both songs were terrible. The gunner Specialist, Neil Perez, from Inwood, Manhattan, who was on his third tour must have heard enough. He yelled for quiet and warned the driver Specialist, Terry Noonan, from Milwaukee that he was following too close behind the lead vehicle. Seconds later the lead Humvee hit an IED, and Noonan started yelling that he had been blinded. When an RPG hit the side of their Humvee, Perez was killed instantly. Mike seemed to be the only one conscious after the second blast. He could hear small arms fire up ahead. Mike took his M4 rifle and climbed out the side of the Humvee. He was almost immediately engaged by Taliban fighters who open fire on him from less than 20 yards. Mike took out 3 of them as the rest retreated into the tree line. He could not believe he had not been hit. Mike could hear an M240 machine gun now letting loose from near the forward Humvee. Then he heard someone yell,

"Hey Badass, what's your situation back there?"

Mike knew it was Sgt. Barrett.

Back home Sgt. Barrett was a heavy equipment operator from Ridgewood, Queens. He had been in the Gulf war. After working on, "The Pile", following 9-11, he re-upped. Sgt. Barrett was much older and more hardened than the rest of the squad. Even more important he seemed fearless and knew his stuff. Mike was happy to hear his voice.

"Not good Sarge, I think Perez is dead and everyone else is in bad shape."

"You think he's dead?" asked Sgt. Barrett.

"He's dead Sarge, he's dead."

"Alright Badass, listen to me, everyone's gone up here. We have no time to grieve, or someone else is going to be grieving all of us. You copy Badass?"

"Copy that Sarge," said Mike.

"I'm gonna make my way back to your position. My leg is torn up. So if I cover you, do you think you can get those men out of that vehicle and behind those rocks on the side of the road?"

"Yes Sir," said Mike

"Alright time to live up to that nickname, let's do this," said Sgt. Barrett.

Now in reality Mike and Sgt Barrett held off over 50 Taliban for almost an hour until help arrived. They saved the lives of Righetti, McKenna, and Noonan. Big Mike Bass would end up at Walter Reed Medical Center. Although he had not realized it, he had been shot multiple times in the initial firefight that day. Big Mike would leave Walter Reed with a Silver Star, Purple Heart, Honorable discharge, and a haunting recurring nightmare.

In Big Mike's dream, Sgt Barrett would be shot and killed making his way back to him. The Taliban fighters would surround his position. Every weapon he picked up would jam. Big Mike would stand up and walk out in the open to the middle of the road. He would hear three shots as Righetti, McKenna, and Noonan were executed. Then the Taliban leader would walk up to Big Mike, point a pistol at his head and everything would go black.

Big Mike was in the midst of his nightmare, but something was very different. In the past, he had always been watching everything unfold. As if he were watching a movie. This time it was first person, everything was exactly as it had been. That was until Sgt Barrett put his machine gun down and calmly walked back to Big Mike's position. He did not hear any gunfire. Sgt Barrett knelt next to him.

"Come on Michael, it's time to put this to rest."

Sgt Barrett helped Big Mike to his feet. They walked around the Humvee to the road. He could see his whole squad standing there completely fine smiling at him. He did not see any Taliban. Sgt Barrett walked with Big Mike up the road past the lead Humvee which sat there completely intact. There was a warm breeze, it was very tranquil.

Sgt. Barrett spoke in a very calm voice.

"You did your job, it's time to mend. He will take you the rest of the way from here Michael."

Big Mike could not believe what he was seeing. He had not seen Elvis in years. Not since he had gone home for the last time with Wyatt. Of all the dogs Big Mike had trained, Elvis had always been his favorite.

"Hey Elvis, what's up man," said Big Mike.

Elvis looked at Big Mike, then turned and started to walk up the road. Big Mike began to cry for the first time in years. He had been so out of touch with his emotions since that day in Afghanistan, that he did not even cry when his mother passed away. Now the tears streamed down his face and it felt good. He could feel himself healing as he followed Elvis up the winding road.

Big Mike sprang awake, he rubbed his eyes which were dry. That was a crazy dream he thought. He got up and took a long shower. On his ride to work that morning he was thinking about his dream. He wondered how Elvis was doing. It must have been seven or eight years since he had seen him last. Elvis would be close to ten years old now. He sent good vibes to Elvis and Wyatt and put the whole thing out of his head.

When Big Mike pulled up to the training facility he saw Janet Cobbler's International parked out front. Janet had moved on from fostering dogs to training them. Big Mike went inside and strolled down the hall. He entered the break room. Janet was sitting at the table reading the newspaper.

"Good Morning Janet, you're early and I see you got my paper," Big Mike said with a smile as he poured himself a cup of coffee.

"Hey Big Mike, yeah Suzanne asked me to come in early. My phone isn't getting a good signal for some reason. So I decided to go old school and read the paper."

"You steal my paper and now you're calling me old?"

Janet laughed, "Pretty sure I'm older than you. Want to hear something funny though. I never read the paper. I'm looking through this one and I see this article. It mentions Elvis, do you remember him? He was in the Rockstar litter years ago. He was the first dog I ever fostered, he was a great dog."

"Yeah, I remember Elvis, I trained him. Let me see that Janet if you will?"

Janet handed Big Mike the paper. There was a picture of Elvis sitting between two young men in football uniforms. Big Mike sat down and started to read the article.

The Adirondak Post
Old Rivalry Renewed
Pine Tree to take on Walnut Heights

It's been 30 years since Glenn Gilmore and, "The Pine Tree Three" lost in the Regional Bowl game to Walnut Heights. People still talk about that game which drew national attention at the time. In the years since Pine Tree has fallen off the map while Walnut Heights has continued its dominance. Because of scheduling changes over the years, Pine Tree no longer plays Walnut Heights during the regular season. However, they will still need to face them in the Regional Bowl game in order to move on to the States. Glenn Gilmore is now an assistant coach for Pine Tree. We interviewed him about this year's undefeated team and their upcoming Bowl game with old rival Walnut Heights.

"I'm extremely proud of this team. Coach Houzer along with Coach Reilly have just done an amazing job here over the past four years. I know it's somewhat cliche to say, but this team really is a family. It starts with those guys at the helm and continues on down the line. We have a great team leader, Tony Connors, who is an All-American center on his way to Oklahoma next year. But really the heart and soul of this team is Wyatt Rule, and his service dog, Elvis. Wyatt who is autistic has been the backup kicker for this team since 8th grade. Much more than that he's really an inspiration. We've all witnessed Wyatt have his personal challenges over the years. He always comes back with a smile on his face. Between him and Elvis, they just bring an incredibly positive vibe. I think with that energy along with the talent on this team and coaching staff, Pine Tree is going to come out on top."

    We also spoke to Pine Tree's All American center, Tony Connors, as he stood alongside his cousin and life long best friend, Wyatt Rule. We asked him about playing with Wyatt and the upcoming game."Wyatt and I have been playing together our whole lives. He's always been a better athlete than me. Back in Middle School I started trying to get him to kick. It was just for fun at first, but he really took to it. People might be surprised but I'd bet he's the best high school kicker in the country. While he's not able to kick all the time, when he does, I've never seen anyone better. He kicked a 70 yarder in practice. We've tried to get him into a few games this year. He hit a 57 yarder against, Willow Creek, which is a school record. I'm so proud of this guy, the obstacles he overcomes every day, and the way he always sees the beauty in everything and everyone always amazes me." Connors finished by giving his prediction for the game. " As far as the game, Walnut Heights does not stand a chance. Wyatt and I have to finish what our fathers could not. This team will not lose."

    Tony Connors's father, Jack, and Wyatt Rule's father, Billy, had rounded out, The Pine Tree Three, along with Glenn Gilmore. Despite them being, All Americans and Gilmore being, All-World, they never beat Walnut Heights. Will this finally be the year? This year's game has been moved back to Pine Tree for the first time since the aforementioned 1990 Bowl game. The game is scheduled to be played next Saturday night at 8 pm. With both teams undefeated, it's shaping up to be a good one.

◆ ◆ ◆

Big Mike finished reading the article and looked up at Janet.

"Sounds like it's going to be a good game. I'll see if my nephew Darryl wants to go with me. Either way, I think I'm going to take a ride down and check it out. Maybe say hello to our old friend Elvis."

"Well if you do go say, hello, for me, I still think about him. He was such a good boy. I'm happy to see he's making a difference."

"Will do Janet," Big Mike Bass said as he sipped his coffee. He knew it seemed crazy. Nevertheless, that game held the key to healing. Now was the time to put the darkness behind him forever.

CHAPTER NINE

Pregame Toast

Tony could see his Uncles and Dad sitting on the front porch as he neared the house. He was with his girlfriend, Kate. It was Saturday afternoon a week before the big game. They were picking up Wyatt on their way to the park. Tony was smiling, because he knew what was coming. He whispered to Kate before they got to the porch.

"These guys are probably gonna bust my chops about the newspaper article and anything else they can think of."

"I can't wait, it should be fun," Kate whispered back.

"Hey, there's Namath now, Broadway Tony. I guarantee a win," said Jack.

Billy chimed in,

"Walnut who??, We got this, forget about it."

This went on for a few minutes, and then Glenn said,

"Don't listen to these two Anthony, they're just jealous because they know you guys are going to do what we could not. Heck, I'd trade one of my Superbowl rings in for another shot at the

Heights."

"Oh boy, here we go again with the SuperBowl rings. What do you have the Heisman in the car," said Jack?

The three of them laughed, the fact was Glenn rarely talked about any of his accomplishments.

"Wyatt should be right out, you going down to the park?" asked Billy.

"Yeah Kate and Wyatt like to go on the new swings while I shoot some hoops," replied Tony.

The Town had installed a steel framed adult-sized swingset, near the basketball courts with Wyatt in mind. He still loved to swing and probably always would. But at 6'6" 210 lbs, he could no longer use the kids' playground. June had approached the town about building a sensory playground for children with autism. It was something she wished they had when Wyatt was little. The town accepted her proposal and one-upped her by adding some adult sensory areas and equipment. Billy and June had suspected that Glenn may have had a hand in that.

Wyatt came bolting out of the house with Elvis by his side. Elvis was still pretty spry and other than a little white fur on his face he looked and moved the same.

Billy called out to Wyatt,

"Hey Wyatt, say Hello to your Uncles."

Wyatt looked over and said, "Hello, hello hello."

Then he gave Tony a high five and took Kate's hand and started off towards the park. Tony laughed, looked at the guys, and said,

"I don't know about these two." Then he turned and said, "Hey wait up."

Billy, Jack, and Glenn were laughing.

Glenn said," Would you look at the size of them."

"Yeah, is Tony bigger than you were senior year Jack?" asked Billy.

"He is taller and 10lbs heavier. He's 6'5, 260, and he swears Wyatts is stronger than him when he uses his strength."

"I don't know about that, but he's definitely very strong," said Billy.

Glenn added, "I'm glad you decided to let him try and kick in games again this year Billy. I know he will probably never be able to kick after high school or on a regular basis. But when he does kick, and I mean this in all sincerity, he's the best I've ever seen."

"Thanks, Glenn, but come on man. Better than pros?" said Billy.

"Yes, on his good days. He has the strongest leg by far that I've ever seen. And his biomechanics are perfect every time. When he's able to focus he is ridiculously accurate and from way out."

"I believe it. I saw him kick that field goal against Willow

Creek. Looked like it was shot out of a cannon," said Jack.

"Yeah well, I'm just glad he enjoys it. The only reason I started letting him kick in games again is that I trust you, Tim, and Frank so much. That and he's built like a piece of steel. I figure if by some small chance he gets hit he won't get hurt anyway."

"Have you decided if he's going to go to the Bowl game yet?" Glenn asked.

"What, you're not gonna let him go to the game?" asked Jack.

"We were thinking about keeping him home. Just because it's going to be such a circus. He struggles sometimes at regular games with everything going on. There's a good chance it may just be too much for him, but we are going to let him go. We've ensured his normal escape route. I'll have the car parked on the service road behind the stands. We've walked through it with Wyatt. If he needs to get out of there he'll tell Molly, "Car". She'll text June and let Elvis off-leash and he will follow Wyatt to the car. He's actually done it before, a few weeks ago I spent the whole first half in the car with him."

"Just out of curiosity, why doesn't Molly just walk with Elvis and Wyatt back to the car?" inquired Jack.

"Because Wyatt sometimes sprints, and no one else can keep up," said Billy.

"He's definitely got your speed, Billy. Is Wyatt going to do another year in school after this?" asked Glenn.

"I think so, he just turned 18 in August and he does not age out of his program until he's 21. So definitely another year. After that, we'll have to see how he's doing."

"I know Anthony is really worried about going away to college next year. He's afraid it's going to affect Wyatt too much. He's even thinking about changing schools and going to Syracuse instead," said Jack.

"Get out of here, I'll talk to Anthony. Listen there's no question that Wyatt is going to miss him, but he'll get over it. He often adapts better than we think. We will just start preparing him for it well ahead of time. It will work out. Now if Kate decides to go with Anthony, Wyatt is probably going to get upset," Billy said with a smile.

They all had a good laugh. Billy reached into the cooler and pulled out 3 beers. Popped them open and passed them out.

"Let's have a toast, that Broadway Tony's prediction comes true, may we finally beat Walnut Heights," Billy said as he raised his beer.

"Here, here," said Glenn and raised his bottle.

"Sla'inte," said Jack as he clinked his bottle off of Billy and Glenn's.

They all took a long swig. Then Glenn said,

"Hey, you guys want to see my Heisman? It's in the car."

They all had another good laugh.

CHAPTER TEN

Game Day

Wyatt sat on top of an old picnic table, with his feet on the bench, eating a piece of Grandma Slevin's pumpkin pie. He was listening to Winkle creek, as it flowed past Slevin's on its way to the Hudson River. Wyatt loved this spot, it was a very close second to the park.

June stood behind the warehouse waiting to talk to her brother, Tommy, who was with a customer. She yelled down the hill to Wyatt.

"Wyatt, make sure you don't give any of that pie to Elvis."

Elvis was lying under the table. He initially sat up when June said his name. Then huffed and put his head down on his paws, as if he knew what she had said. It was a constant battle to keep Wyatt from sharing his snacks with Elvis. Wyatt did not acknowledge June. Besides he had already given Elvis half when she wasn't looking.

Tommy finished up with the customer and walked over to June.

"Hey June, sorry to bother you today. I know the big game is tonight, but I can't get into the system and access the inventory or order anything for that matter."

June was still heavily involved in the running of Slevins. Although she worked mostly from home.

"No worries Tommy, you know Wyatt loves it here. Just keep an eye on him, while I check it out."

"No problem, Paul and Debra are working up front. So I'll just chill with my man Wyatt, I got something for him anyway."

Tommy was holding a brown paper bag.

"What's that? Don't give him any candy or anything."

"Relax, I would never give him something to eat without checking with you first. I know he has allergies. It's not food, you'll see when you come out it's no big deal."

June gave Tommy half a smirk, shook her head, and went into the warehouse. When she came back out Wyatt had his back to her. He was throwing stones into the creek, one of his favorite pastimes.

Tommy was smiling, he looked at June and said,

"I wasn't sure if he'd like them or not but so far he seems happy."

As June got closer she could see that Wyatt was wearing a pair of gold Elvis-style sunglasses.

"Why'd you get him those?" asked June.

"Don't you remember when Wyatt first got Elvis someone gave him a pair of cheap Elvis Presley novelty sunglasses?"

"Yes, I remember he wore them all the time until they broke. I got him another pair but he would not wear them. In fact, he won't wear sunglasses period. What made you think of getting him those?"

"I was talking to Billy, he said that he thinks the lights at the night games bother Wyatt's eyes. They tried to get him a tinted visor for his Helmet but he won't wear that either. So I saw these and I figured it was worth a try."

"Those don't look like novelty glasses, Tommy? I hope you didn't spend a lot of money on them?"

"They weren't too expensive, but they are the real deal. I wanted them to protect his eyes, those cheap ones don't. Besides, look at him, he really does play them off. He looks really cool. You like those glasses, Wyatt?"

Wyatt smiled big and in a sing-song voice he sometimes used said,

"S-u-n-g-l-a-s-s-e-s."

Jack walked into his house and kicked his sneakers off. He had just got back from a morning jog. He was on his way upstairs to take a shower when he heard a familiar song blasting from the basement stereo. It was, "Rainbow in the Dark," by Dio. Anthony played Jack's old CDs when he lifted weights. Jack headed down to the basement to check it out. Sure enough, Anthony was stretching getting ready to lift. Jack turned the music off.

"What are you doing, you're working out?" said Jack.

"I was going to, I have all this nervous energy."

"Well take my advice, don't. You'll regret it come game time. Do your stretching then maybe go for a walk or something to take your mind off the game, but don't go crazy exercising now. If you do, your legs will be dead later. Trust me, I did it to myself a few times and almost lost matches to guys I should have easily beat."

"Alright, that makes sense. I just wish the game was now. Are you going with mom and Winnie later?" replied Anthony.

"Yes, I'm taking your Aunt June too. Your Uncle is heading over early so he can park the car on the service road for Wyatt. I'm also picking up Mr. Gilmore."

"Wow, Mr. Gilmore is coming? He hasn't made it to a game all year."

"Yeah well he's been having some health issues, but he'd have to be dead before he'd miss this game. You know he was the driving force in getting the bowl games back to Pine Tree," said Jack.

"What's the deal with him and Walnut Heights? I know everyone is into the rivalry, but it seems really personal to him."

Jack laughed, "Don't kid yourself, it's personal for a lot of us. You're right though his distaste for Walnut Heights is deeply ingrained. As far as I know, it goes back a long way. Something to do with him and the man who was the mayor there forever. I've asked your Uncle Glenn, but if he knows he's not telling."

"Well I'm sure Mr. Gilmore has his reasons," said Anthony.

"I agree, Mr. Gilmore is a good man. I've never seen him treat anyone unfairly. He's always been especially good to us and everyone in this town for that matter. Now try to forget about the game for a few hours. Go outside and enjoy the weather, it's unseasonably warm today."

"I'll try Dad, but I really hope we win tonight."

"I hope you guys win too. Just go out and play your game. That's all you can do. When it's all said and done you know what the two most important things are?"

"I know Dad, Family, and friends."

"That's right, in that order. And don't ever let anyone tell you differently. I love you, buddy."

"Alright now you're getting weird," said Tony.

"Why what's wrong? Come on, ya big lug, give your old man a hug."

Jack was laughing as he pretended he was going to bear hug Tony.

Tony yelled, "Get away from me ya big weirdo."

Jack laughed harder and patted Tony's head.

"Alright I'll see you later, I have to shower. Remember what I told you, don't wear yourself out now."

Jack went back up the stairs. Tony felt better, more relaxed, and confident. He did his best professional wrestling flex in the mirror and said,

"You're going down Walnut Heights."

Big Mike and his nephew Darryl rolled into Pine tree two hours before kickoff. He figured there would be some traffic, but nothing like this, the town was packed. Everything was green and white. As they neared the High School they were directed to keep driving. The upper parking lots were already full.

"They are really into their football around here," said Darryl.

Just then two people in Pine tree costumes followed by a third dressed as an Eagle ran across the road in front of them. Big Mike and Darryl laughed.

"Well that's something you didn't think you'd see when you woke up this morning," Big Mike said as he looked over at Darryl.

"Yeah an Eagle, chasing two toilet brushes."

Big Mike smiled, "Those were Pine Trees man."

Darryl laughed, "I know, hey Uncle Mike this is the first time we went anywhere and I was old enough to ride in the front seat."

"Sorry about that Darryl, we have to do stuff more often, that's on me."

"I didn't mean anything by it, Uncle Mike, just that I'm getting older. But I'll take you up on the offer."

"Alright, that's a deal, little man."

Big Mike parked the car in a makeshift lot that looked to be baseball fields. They could see all the lights lit up around the football field up on the hill.

"That's a lot of lights for a High School football field," said Big Mike.

"Yeah I thought I saw a jumbotron when we drove by too," replied Darryl.

"Alright let's go check it out, see if we can find my old friend Elvis I was telling you about."

Molly was playing fetch with Elvis on the practice football field. Wyatt was in the locker room with the team. Tony would text her when the team was ready to come out. She would then hang back with Wyatt and walk out with him a little while after. This was a result of trial and error. Wyatt had initially come out with the team and was overwhelmed by all the pregame hype. This had led to another pregame ritual. Wyatt would walk out after and sit at his own bench. Each player one by one would make their way over, give him a high five, and pet Elvis for good luck. The tradition seemed to be working. They hadn't lost a home game in two years.

Big Mike and Darryl followed some of the crowd. They made their way up a dirt trail towards the main field. As they crested the top of the hill Big Mike saw a woman playing with a dog in a field off to their left. He knew that dog was Elvis.

"Hey Darryl that looks like Elvis over there, let's go see."

Elvis saw Big Mike heading towards him. He should have been surprised but he wasn't. He had been thinking about Big Mike a lot lately. He felt his presence now before he even came into view. Elvis knew what he needed to do. He did not know why, that was unimportant.

"Hello there, is that Elvis fetching that ball?" Big Mike said to Molly.

"Yes it is, you know Elvis?" asked Molly.

"I sure do, I'm sorry my name is Mike Bass. I trained Elvis for Wyatt. I thought you might be June when I came walking up."

Elvis came jogging back with the Tennis ball.

"Oh no, I'm Wyatts 1-1, Molly."

Elvis came over to Big Mike now.

"Is he working or can I pet him?" Big Mike knew that Elvis wasn't currently working but he wanted to be respectful.

"Of course, he's not on duty yet. We have to go get Wyatt soon though."

Big Mike knelt down gingerly on one knee and started to pet Elvis.

"What's up Elvis, how are you, man? You're getting old like me. Look at that white face, old man. How's he been doing with Wyatt?" Big Mike asked Molly.

"He is great with Wyatt, could not be better."

"This is my nephew Darryl." Darryl came closer and petted Elvis.

Elvis dropped the Tennis ball at Darryl's feet. Molly said,

"Hi Darryl, you can throw him the ball if you want."

Darryl said, "OK, thanks."

He picked the ball up and threw it. Elvis took off after it. When Elvis got to the ball he picked it up and sat down. Molly looked a little stunned.

"He's never done that before."

She called him.

"Elvis come", ``ELVIS COME!"

But instead of running back, Elvis laid down.

"That is so strange, he always comes back," said Molly.

"It's probably my fault, I'm sure I threw him off," replied Big Mike.

They all started to walk towards Elvis who was still lying down. As they got within 20 feet Elvis got up and started walking further ahead. Big Mike picked up his pace a little to go and get him.

"Elvis Wait," said Big Mike.

As Big Mike got closer he had a quick flash of following Elvis in his dream. Big Mike shook his head. He felt a little weird and hoped no one had noticed. Elvis stopped and sat again. Big Mike knelt next to him.

"Where are you going Elvis, listen it was good to see you, but I think it's time for me to say goodbye. It's nice to see you've been doing so well all these years. I'm proud of you man and so is Janet, she told me to say, hello."

Molly and Darryl were standing there now. Molly snapped the leash back on Elvis.

"That was so strange, I don't know what got into him. Well, it was nice to meet you guys. I'll tell Billy and June you said Hi."

"It was nice to meet you too Molly, goodbye Elvis." Big Mike said.

He started to turn towards the gate that led to the service road behind the stands. Just then Elvis barked, looked at Big Mike, and then looked towards the fence that was between them and the service road. Then he started to walk away with Molly to retrieve her backpack which she had forgotten on the other side of the field.

"I guess he's saying goodbye," Molly said as she waved to Big

Mike and Darryl.

Big Mike smiled and waved. Then he turned to Darryl.

"Hey Darryl, listen, man, Why don't you run over and get on that concession line. Get us a couple of hotdogs, I'll take an ice tea and whatever you want. I have to make a quick phone call. I can see you from here." He handed Darryl some money.

"No worries Uncle Mike, I'm 13 now. I think I can handle it."

Big Mike watched Darryl run over and get online. Then he turned his focus back towards the spot where Elvis had been looking. A man had been standing there a moment ago but now he didn't see him. There were a lot of other people walking on the road. Big Mike walked up to the 4ft high chain-link fence, he felt a warm breeze. He closed his eyes for a second, and someone said, "Badass?"

Big Mike turned to his right and saw a man standing there holding a two-way radio. It took a second and then it clicked, Joe Righetti.

"Righetti? What the hell are you doing here?" Big Mike said with a huge grin.

"Badass, I thought that was you, this is crazy. I've been up here for about 12 years now. What brings you here?

"I train service dogs up near Lake Placid. I saw an article about this game in the paper and thought my nephew would like to check it out. What about you?"

"I went back to school at The University of Albany when I got out of the VA. Met my wife out one night, she went to Siena, she grew up in Pine Tree. We got married and I've been here ever since. I'm the head of buildings and grounds for the Pine Tree school district."

"That's great man, you look good."

"You know I still talk to McKenna from time to time. That's why this is so crazy. I just talked to him the other night. Unfortunately, he had bad news. Sgt. Barrett passed away recently, he had cancer."

Big Mike was taken back a little. He felt himself well up for a second, then it passed.

"Oh man, I had no idea. That's terrible, how long was he sick?"

"McKenna said he wasn't sure. But he thinks for a while. You know he was in the Gulf and then worked on the pile after 9-11. A lot of people have gotten sick from being in those places. Knowing Sgt. Barrett, I'm sure he battled to the end."

"No doubt, there was nobody tougher. How's McKenna doing?"

"He's good, still a little crazy but doing well. He and his brother own the largest RV dealership in Arkansas. He's married with 6 kids. His oldest boy is actually a really good baseball player. He's being recruited by all the big schools, but he may just go in the draft."

"How about you, any kids?" asked Big Mike.

"Yeah 3 girls, I pray every day they don't bring home a guy like me."

Big Mike laughed, "Nah, come on they could do a lot worse. What about Noonan?"

"Nobody knows last I heard he was in Boston.

Hey let me give you my cell and McKenna's if you don't mind I'm sure he would love to hear from you," said Righetti.

Big Mike and Righetti exchanged numbers. Big Mike reached out and shook his hand.

"It was great to see you. So sorry to hear about Sgt. Barrett though. If you hear anything about a memorial or benefit for him let me know."

Righetti gave him a thumbs up and said, "I will."

Big Mike waved then turned to find Darryl.

Righetti called out, "Hey Mike", Big Mike turned back to face him.

"Thank You man, you saved our lives."

Big Mike could see Righetti had tears in his eyes.

"I don't know what to say to that Joe."

"You don't have to say anything, just know it's true. And know this, if you ever need anything don't hesitate to call. I mean that brother, anything."

Big Mike nodded his head and said,

"Thank you, be good, brother."

He turned again and saw Darryl waiting for him near the gate. When he got closer Darryl asked,

"Who was that guy?"

"That was the oracle, Joe Righetti." Big Mike said with a little smile.

"Who?" replied Darryl.

"An old friend, let's go watch some football. This should be a good game.

CHAPTER ELEVEN

More than a game

The team gathered in the gymnasium for their pregame pep talk. Glenn and Coach Reilly had already spoken. It was now Coach Houzer's turn. He had practiced his talk at home for the past week. It was going to be epic. A real "Win one for the Gipper," with the Town of Pine Tree being, "The Gipper." The speech was going well. Coach Houzer had been holding off on mentioning Walnut Heights until near his dramatic ending. Then they would charge out of the school and storm the field.

"THAT'S NOT just any team over there. That's WALNUT HEIGHTS!"

Coach Houzer paused for dramatic effect. When from the rear of the gym came an unexpected voice. Wyatt using Tony's inflection of the TV sound effect yelled,

"DUN, DUN, DUUUUN!"

The whole gym broke out in laughter. Coach Houzer even had to laugh. When things calmed he said,

"Thanks for that Wyatt. He's got the right idea. You guys know what we have to do. We all know we can beat Walnut Heights. So let's go out and play our game. Walnut Heights is just an obstacle on our way to a State Championship. So play smart, play hard, and let's have some fun. LET'S GO!"

Pine Tree took the field. Because it was the Regional Bowl game there was a lot more pregame ceremony. When the dust settled Wyatt nonchalantly walked out with Elvis and Molly.

"Billy, Tommy, look, Wyatt has his Elvis sunglasses on," said June.

"He looks pretty calm so far, maybe they are helping. Good call Tommy," replied Billy.

"Thanks, and he looks cool," said Tommy.

The program had said that Wyatt was number 3. So far Big Mike had not seen him or Elvis on the sideline. Then Big Mike spotted Wyatt walking out.

"That's Wyatt there, Oh man look at the size of him. He was just a little boy the last time I saw him. And check out his shades," Big Mike laughed.

"There's Elvis too," said Darryl.

Big Mike and Darryl watched as each player gave Wyatt a high five and petted Elvis.

"That's pretty cool, a real family, good to see," said Big Mike.

"Yeah pretty cool," replied Darryl.

Pine Tree won the coin toss and decided to defer so they would get the ball to start the second half. Then the worst possible thing happened: Walnut Heights ran the opening kickoff back 89 yards for a TD. Pine Tree went three and out on their opening drive. Walnut Heights scored another TD on the next possession. They always went for a two-point conversion after a TD. So far it had been working, Walnut Heights converted on both of their attempts. The score at the end of the first quarter was Walnut Heights 16 Pine Tree 0.

Tim Houzer knew he needed to change something up quickly. Tony had tweaked his knee playing defense at the end of his junior year. Jack told him at the time to pick one position and stick with it. Tony chose to play Center. Although he had been a very good Defensive End. A week before the Bowl game Tim spoke to Jack about possibly letting Tony play at DE if they were in trouble. Jack had agreed to let Anthony play on both sides of the ball, as needed through the end of the season. That time had come, they needed to shake things up.

The move paid off right away. Tony sacked the Walnut Heights quarterback for a big loss to start the second quarter. They went three and out for the first time. Pine Tree had good field position and Kenny Austin was able to hit a 38-yard field goal. Tony continued to wreak havoc on Walnut Heights. Just before the half, he caused a fumble. Pine Tree recovered and scored a TD on the ensuing drive.

The score was now Walnut Heights 16 Pine Tree 10. As the half came to a close June got a text from Molly.

Molly: Wyatt is starting to get very busy.

June: OK, do you want us to come get him?

Molly: I just asked him again if he wants to leave. He

said, car, car, car.

June: Alright, Billy will meet you by the car

Molly: Ok, we are on our way.

Billy met Wyatt, Elvis, and Molly by the car. Wyatt got into the back seat followed by Elvis.

"He started to get very busy. He had his finger in his ear and was saying something over and over under his breath," said Molly.

"Yeah no worries Molly, thank you. I'm just gonna chill with him in the car for a while. If he wants to go back to the field or leave, I'll text you either way."

"Okay, I will be close by"

"Sounds good."

Billy got in the driver's seat, and Wyatt was quiet.

"Do you want to go home, Wyatt?"

Wyatt did not answer.

"It's not a big deal, we can go whenever you want. Just tell me, home."

Wyatt did not say anything.

"Do you just want to hang out in the car for a while?"

"Hang out, hang out, hang out," replied Wyatt.

"Alright buddy, we will just hang out then."

Billy texted June to let her know what was going on. Then he tried to put the game on the radio, but this seemed to bother Wyatt so he turned it off. He could see one of the scoreboards from where he was parked. They stayed in the car for the entire halftime. The third quarter started and Wyatt seemed content in the back seat. He was eating snacks and doing puzzles on his iPad as Elvis slept. Billy heard the crowd get very loud and then his phone blew up with texts. Before he checked his phone he watched the scoreboard. Pine Tree 16, then 17 with the extra point, Walnut Heights 16. It was short lived however just before the end of the third, Walnut Heights scored again and converted another two-point conversion. Going into the fourth the score was Walnut Heights 24 Pine Tree 17.

Billy asked Wyatt again if he wanted to go home. Wyatt surprised him when he said,

"Game."

"You want to go back to the game?" asked Billy.

Wyatt said very fast, "Go back to the game, game, game."

"Alright, no problem man. They could use some good mojo from you and Elvis anyway."

Billy texted Molly and she came and got Wyatt and Elvis. To

Billy's surprise, he heard some pretty loud cheers when they got back to the sidelines. Shortly after Pine Tree scored another TD. Pine Tree 24 Walnut Heights 24. In the next few series, neither team really moved the ball. Then with about 6 minutes left in the game, Walnut Heights scored another TD. This time they kicked the extra point. Making it Walnut Heights 31 Pine Tree 24. Pine Tree went three and out on their next possession. Then Tony took a page out of his father's book. On the next Walnut Heights drive, he knocked the ball loose right to one of his teammates. Kevin Whittle ran the ball back 66 yards for a TD. The crowd went crazy. At that moment like clockwork, Pine Trees' old demons revisited. Kenny Austin who had not missed an extra point in 2 seasons did just that. Walnut Heights 31 Pine Tree 30.

Pine Tree was not ready to give up just yet. Coach Reilly along with Glenn and Tony riled up the troops. They stopped Walnut Heights from just running out the clock. With time winding down Walnut Heights had to punt. They pinned Pine Tree deep in their own end with just over 2 minutes left and 1 timeout. Pine Tree was able to move the ball but in small chunks. With time ticking away they converted a pass down to the Walnut Heights 46, they were kept in bounds. Timeout was called with 6 seconds left in the game. Pine Tree had two options. A Hail Mary pass or a 63-yard field goal. It looked bleak to most in attendance except for Tony Connors.

Tony immediately ran up to Coach Houzer to convince him to let Wyatt try a field goal. Kenny Austin who had never hit anything further than a 53 yarder, was in agreement. So was most of the team. Even the QB, Otto Secor, thought they had a better chance if Wyatt kicked, rather than one shot at the end zone. The million-dollar question was, could they even get Wyatt to kick? Coach Houzer waved over Glenn and Coach Reilly for their input.

"Do you think you can get him out there in all this noise safely

Anthony? Glenn asked.

"Absolutely"

"Then listen, give it a shot. You and Kenny know Wyatt. So if you don't think he's gonna kick, DO NOT SNAP the ball. Take the delay of game penalty, then we'll have to try for the Hail Mary. Otto has a strong enough arm, 5 more yards is not going to make a big difference."

They all agreed with Glenn, although Tony had not needed any convincing. Glenn waved up to Billy in the stands. When he got his attention he pointed to his phone. Then he called him.

"What's up Glenn?"

"Just wanted to give you a heads up. We are gonna give Wyatt a shot at kicking a field goal here."

"Oh, I don't know if that's a good idea, Glenn. All this noise and he's having a tough time tonight."

"Do you want me to stop them?" asked Glenn.

Billy could see Anthony already getting Wyatt onto the field.

Billy sighed, "No, let him try. Just do me a favor and tell Molly that I will be by the car if anything goes wrong."

"You got it, brother," said Glenn.

Billy hung up and told June and Jack what was going on. Mr. Gilmore was sitting behind them and overheard Billy. He leaned forward and said in a loud voice,

"He's gonna hit it." He laughed a little and looked at Billy this time and said it again. "He's gonna hit it, Billy."

"I believe you, Mr. Gilmore, thanks," said Billy as he took off towards the car.

Big Mike and Darryl were on the edge of their seats. They had really been enjoying the game.

"Look, Uncle Mike, I think Wyatts going in the game."

"Oh man, I think you're right. I remember reading that he can hit some crazy long-field goals. But I'm surprised they'd try and let him kick in this atmosphere.

"I hope he hits it," said Darryl.

"Me too, that would be something to see."

Tony was starting to feel a little uneasy about putting Wyatt in this situation as he walked with him onto the field.

The crowd erupted in cheers when they realized Wyatt was going in. Tony could see that Wyatt was squinting and putting his finger in the earhole on his helmet.

"It's Okay Wyatt, just like practice man. You can hit this.

Are you ready?"

Wyatt did not answer, Tony was hoping for an OK, OK, OK or

a kick, kick, kick. He would have settled for one OK. Getting nothing along with the physical stims was not good. Tony instructed Kenny to ask Wyatt one more time if he was ready to kick once they lined up. If Wyatt said anything other than "kick" or "OK" he was to yell No to Tony. Tony would not snap the ball and they would take the penalty.

Kenny assured Tony not to worry. He had been the one who flipped Wyatt the ball back in Eighth grade. He wasn't going to make that mistake again. Kenny was Wyatt's holder ever since. He knew when Wyatt was going to kick, maybe even better than Tony.

Billy was waiting by the car. He really thought he was going to puke this time. He heard someone call down to him from atop the bleachers.

"Mr. Rule, Mr. Rule, up here, It's me, Johnny Lopez."

Billy smiled, he knew Johnny Lopez well. Johnny had been in many of Wyatt's classes when they were little. Johnny had Asperger's, he was a sweet kid. He was also very smart and knew everything about sports.

"Hey Johnny, how are you?"

Johnny said he was good, then started rattling off percentages and odds of Wyatt hitting the Field goal. He had also informed Billy that a 63 yarder would tie the NY state record set in 1990. Billy cut Johnny off and yelled up to him.

"Johnny can you just let me know when he kicks it?"

"Absolutely, I can do that. Absolutely, I would be happy to do that," replied Johnny.

"Thank you, Johnny."

"They're lining up now," Johnny called down to Billy.

Kenny asked Wyatt if he was ready, but he already could see that Wyatt was not going to kick. Wyatt was holding his hands in front of his face mask. Kenny yelled to Tony,

"NO, NO, NO!"

Tony let the play clock run out. Pine Tree was called for delay of game and took the 5-yard penalty. Then inexplicably, Walnut Heights called a time out. Nobody was sure why. Maybe they were trying to ice Wyatt. Walnut Heights was aware that Wyatt had a very strong leg. Tony went over to Wyatt to see if he was alright.

"It's okay Wyatt, good try man."

"S-U-N-G-L-A-S-S-E-S," Wyatt said to Tony.

"If I get your sunglasses to wear under your helmet will you kick?" asked Tony.

"Kick, kick, kick, Sunglasses," Wyatt replied. He was smiling now as he held his head down and squinted his eyes.

"Stay here Wyatt, I'll be right back."

Tony sent Kenny to get Wyatt's sunglasses off Molly.

Johnny called down to Billy again.

"Wyatt didn't kick, they got a delay of game. That's a five-yard penalty."

Billy shook his head. He just hoped Wyatt wasn't struggling.

"Did Wyatt come off the field yet Johnny?" Billy yelled.

"No, he's still out there," Johnny paused. Then said,

"Looks like Kenny Austin just gave Wyatt his sunglasses. I think he's going to kick. That would be a new state record, 68 yards."

Billy shook his head again. He thought to himself, this is crazy.

"Alright Johnny, let me know what happens."

"You told me that already Mr. Rule, I got it," said Johnny.

Billy smiled, "Sorry Johnny, you're right."

Tony ran over to tell Coach Houzer that Wyatt was still going to kick.

"I don't know Tony, that would be 68 yarder now," said Coach Houzer.

"If he was gonna hit it from 63, he'll hit it from 68. Whenever he kicks like that he has plenty of distance. Come on, you've seen him hit 70 yarders on this field before," pleaded Tony.

Coach Reilly agreed with Tony that Wyatt had the leg to do it.

Glenn chimed in that he still thought it was their best chance.

"Alright let's go for it."

Tony quickly ran back onto the field before they changed their minds. Wyatt was already wearing his shades under his helmet.

"You good to kick Wyatt?" asked Tony.

Wyatt didn't say anything, but he gave Tony a big smile.

"Alright let's do this, same as before Kenny," said Tony.

They lined up to kick. Kenny looked back at Wyatt; he definitely looked more focused.

Johnny yelled down to Billy, "They're lining up now!"

Billy had a lump in his throat. An eerie silence fell over the crowd.

"Are you okay to kick, Wyatt?" Kenny asked.

Wyatt did not respond, Kenny yelled again,

"ARE YOU OKAY TO KICK WYATT?"

Tony was getting nervous. He could hear what was going on behind him as the play clock ticked away. Then he heard Wyatt say," OK, OK, OK," followed immediately by Kenny screaming.

"READY!"

Tony snapped the ball. He usually heard the sound of the kick shortly after. Something seemed wrong. Then just when he thought they wouldn't be able to hold the rush any longer. Tony heard the loudest thud imaginable. He looked up and caught a glimpse of the ball rocketing end over end into the night sky.

Billy heard a loud thud and then saw the football high above the lights. The crowd erupted with an incredible roar.

Johnny Lopez screamed down to Billy,

"HE HIT IT, MR. RULE...HE HIT IT, MR. RULE...

IT WOULD HAVE BEEN GOOD FROM 80!"

Tony's teammates were jumping on him yelling,

"IT'S GOOD, HE HIT IT!"

Tony pulled away to check on Wyatt, just in time to see him sprinting off the other end of the field. He had his helmet off, his arms up, and his hands flapping as he ran. Tony could see Elvis running from the sideline to catch up. He fought through the crowd to get to Wyatt.

Billy saw Wyatt running off the field onto the track and through the gate to the service road. Elvis was at his side. He could see the lights shining off Wyatt's gold sunglasses.

Billy was crying and laughing at the same time. He said out loud to himself as Wyatt ran towards him,

"Elvis has left the building."

Billy opened the rear car door. Wyatt gave him a high five and jumped into the back seat followed by Elvis. Billy could see Anthony making his way towards him with June in tow.

"How is he?" asked Tony.

"He was smiling when he jumped in the back seat. I think he may just be a little over-stimulated. How are you? That was unbelievable," said Billy.

"It still hasn't sunk in yet, listen to that. Everyone is still going nuts out there."

June was talking to Molly, then she came over.

"That was insane Billy, you should have seen that kick. The ball must be in the woods somewhere. It just kept going," said June.

She walked around to the passenger's side of the car and opened Wyatt's door to see how he was. Tony walked over. June stepped back to let him see Wyatt. Tony leaned into the car.

"That was unbelievable man. You did it, that was the greatest kick anyone ever saw. Good job Wyatt."

Wyatt smiled and said,

"Shake, shake, shake."

Tony and June laughed.

"He wants to get a shake Billy," said June.

"Sounds good to me, let's get out of here. Anthony, great game man. Really, I mean it, very impressive. Now don't celebrate too hard. You still have two left for that State Championship."

Billy gave Tony a hug and patted him on the shoulder pads. Tony half turned to head back and said,

"Thanks, Uncle Billy, Thanks, Aunt June. Great job Wyatt! I have to go find that ball."

Billy got in the car. The three of them and Elvis drove down the service road behind the school and out onto the backcountry roads. The town of Pine Tree celebrated behind them.

It was a long drive home. Big Mike and Darryl stopped at the Diner on the way. They were both pumped up when they left the game. Big Mike kept saying that he could not believe what he had seen. Darryl agreed it was like some kind of movie. He told Big Mike that the kick had gone viral on social media. It was late by the time he dropped Darryl off at home.

Big Mike was drained when he finally got into his house. He washed up and brushed his teeth. He was still thinking about Wyatt's kick as he sat on the corner of his bed.

Big Mike had not really thought about the conversation with Joe Righetti until now. He started to think about all the guy's in his squad. If it was true what Righetti had said, it was also true that Sgt. Barrett's coolness under fire had given Big Mike the confidence to do great things that day. Without him, none of them would have made it. Big Mike closed his eyes. He could see Sgt. Barrett in his dream saying,

"You did your job, It's time to mend."

Big Mike thought about his mother. How he had been so afraid of his emotions, he had not allowed himself to properly grieve her loss. How he lied to himself about being stronger than the darkness. The emotion came to a head and tears streamed down Big Mike's face. He sobbed for it all.

When he thought he could cry no more. He pictured that little boy he had met years ago on the training facility porch. He reveled in the fact that one little autistic boy could bring happiness to so many. He thought of Wyatt and Elvis and cried tears of joy.

Big Mike finally got under his covers feeling truly at peace for the first time in many years. His eyes grew very heavy as he whispered,

"Thank You, Elvis."

He fell into a deep sleep. The darkness was gone.

CHAPTER TWELVE

A Quiet Victory

Billy and June stood in the park as Wyatt swung on the swings. June was watching some crows chase a red-tailed hawk across the sky.

"Man, those crows are really giving that hawk a tough time," said June.

"That's their job, it's part of the deal they have with the squirrels," replied Billy.

June laughed, "What are you talking about?"

"You don't know? The crows have a deal with the squirrels. They protect the squirrels from the hawks. In turn, the squirrels let the crows eat their dead."

June laughed harder, "You're out of your mind, where do you come up with this stuff?"

Billy couldn't hold a straight face, he smiled and said,

"It's common knowledge June, just ask the squirrels."

They had the park to themselves, most of the town was at the

State Championship game in Syracuse. Wyatt had seldom gone to away games. It was often too much for him to handle. The state tournament was played in the Carrier Dome, a.k.a "The loud house." Billy and June had taken Wyatt there once as a toddler, he lasted all of about ten minutes. So when he did not seem interested in going to the games they were actually relieved. Pine Tree had crushed their opponent in the state semi-final 49-10.

Billy's phone buzzed, it was a text from Jack.

Jack: Broadway Tony made good on his prediction.

The Pine Tree Eagles are the new State Champions.

Billy: That's good news man. Tell everyone we said

congratulations.

Jack: They could not have done it without Wyatt.

Billy: I'll let him know. Thanks, Jack, I'll talk to you

later, enjoy.

Billy told June about Pine Tree's big win. Then he yelled over to Wyatt who was swinging in the opposite direction.

"HEY, WYATT YOUR TEAM WON! THE PINE TREE EAGLES ARE THE NEW STATE CHAMPIONS! YOU DID IT BUDDY!"

Wyatt Rule smiled wide as he swung in the park with Elvis by his side. Back in Syracuse, Tony Connors dedicated the State Championship to Wyatt and raised the trophy high over his head.

It was a beautiful fall day. Wyatt had a peaceful, easy feeling, as he looked out over the endless fields of green grass.

ACKNOWLEDGMENTS

This book would not have been possible without my wife Tara. Thank you for always dropping everything to read and edit my drafts. More importantly for being a fierce advocate and great mom to William. We appreciate and love you very much. To our family and friends for being curious, and supportive over the years, not critical and judging, thank you. To my son for helping me to see the true beauty in all the sights, sounds, and energy around us. Who never gets caught up in the nonsense that we are all inundated with. You have taught me so much. I love you, William, thank you.

Finally, I would like to say don't stop including or inviting those families you know with special needs children to your parties or events. They may not have shown up to so many things by now that you've given up. Keep asking, they may surprise you sometime. Many people raising children with special needs can become more and more isolated especially as the children grow older. This all too often can lead to a situation where you have an elderly parent being the only caregiver. Inclusion is so very important because it helps to create a lifelong support system. If you think of anyone you know that's caring for someone with special needs, check in on them. It's never too late to lend a hand or even just some moral support. To those of you who are caring for someone with special needs don't be afraid to ask for help. You may be surprised how many people are willing to but don't know how.

While thoughts and prayers are warm and fuzzy. Actions are what truly make a difference.

AUTHOR

Jeff Conlan lives in Putnam County, N.Y.

With his wife, Tara, son William and

William's service dog Charger.

Made in United States
North Haven, CT
29 April 2022

18711729R10088